13.00
'24

The Dazzle of the Light

Patrick Hegarty

The Dazzle of the Light

Wexford College Press

MENS SANA INCORPORE SANO

Printed as a Wexford College Press hardcover 2003
by arrangement with Watchmaker Publishing Ltd.

ISBN 1-929148-15-1

Original paperback ISBN 0-9709917-7-0
Library of Congress Control Number: 2001098979

Wexford College Press
www.WexfordCollegePress.com
Books@WexfordCollegePress.com

Printed and bound in the United States of America

0 9 8 7 6 5 4 3 2 1

For John

Long enough have you dreamed contemptible dreams,

Now I wash the gum from your eyes,

You must habit yourself to the dazzle of the light

and of every moment of your life

–Walt Whitman

The Pub

ONE

Because they have their noses stuck in books half their lives, some brainiacs just *know* things. Useless crap, like when the Magna Carta was signed, what the square root of 102 is, how many protons are buzzing around in the middle of some friggin' cell. But I was never much of a scholar. I only graduated high school because Mr. Mayhew felt bad that my mom was dying and he couldn't stomach another year of what he called, "My flippant disregard for all things academic." He was right, though. I just couldn't sit and listen to some burned-out loser like Ms. Parsons lecture about the importance of Freud's dream theory while my mom was being eaten alive at Tryon Municipal Hospital only a couple miles away. No, the life of the mind never appealed to me. I always trusted my appetites, let my spleen, heart, and guts lead the way.

That's why, at this particular moment, the dude's name slips my mind. But I'm pretty sure that *some* Roman or Greek, a Titicus or Senecus, once said that an unexamined life isn't worth living. I don't know if that's true, but I do know that an *over*-examined life can't be lived at all. Some people over-science things, think so much they forget to live. When invited to a party, most people wanna know when and where, but others can't help but ask, "Why?"

This story is about my brother, Liam, a guy who's been asking why most of his life. Night after night, he sits in this dank North Denver bar, drinking his Murphy's, questioning the cosmos, writing story after story about our past. Wasting away, like a loser. That's him at the table by the window, the black-haired guy with the freckles and the glasses. Yeah, the one scribbling like a madman in that

9

notebook, a dog-eared copy of *Leaves of Grass* in his hand. For some reason, Liam thinks the key to his life is buried somewhere in books and the minutiae of our family history, so he pores over details, dissecting them one by one, in the belief that sense can be made out of destiny. I know it's crazy and you know it's crazy, but Liam thinks that by examining the past he'll be able to secure some kind of future. I try to tell him that nothin' in this life has been secured yet–that there's no such thing as tomorrow, just an endless string of todays–but for the last eighteen months the kid's had some trouble hearing me. He's been listening to a tyrannical French midget instead.

This bar, Rainbow Street South, boasts of specializing in Greek, Italian, and Mexican food, but judging by the pained faces of the belching customers seated throughout, I'd say that heartburn, indigestion, and drunkenness would be a little more like it. The sample platter–with its greasy microwaved tacos, oozing fried cheese sticks, and floury gyros–is enough to make even the strongest of stomachs rebel. I used to be able to eat jalapenos like peanuts, but even *I* wouldn't think about ordering the enchiladas with *habanero* sauce here. The soiled bar napkin beneath Liam's pint displays the slogan it took Rainbow Street's owner and bartender, Dick Hackett, a month and a half to come up with. The fruit of all that thinking? His 45 days of brainstorming, racking his brain to come up with the most succinct and appealing slogan he could muster?

"RAINBOW STREET SOUTH–WHERE DRINKING MAKES YOU COLORFUL."

Genius, huh? But as I take a look at Tracy and Bart Morris and the others slouched at the bar–the glassy eyes, nicotine-stained lips, and blank stares–I'd have to say that drinking does just the opposite. Judging by these jokers, I'd say that drinking just sucks the color right out of you.

Dick and his gay lover of ten years, Tracy, haven't quite figured that out yet. They still throw 'em down with a vengeance, hoping the color will eventually come. By the way, I'm not shittin' you, those are their names: Tracy and Dick, Dick and Tracy. Dick-Tracy. I know the jokes are obvious, but I can't resist. I've often thought that, together, Dick and Tracy could be a couple of homosexual comic-book crime fighters, wearing yellow trench coats, prancing through the inner city and talking into their fashionable wristwatches while battling bad fashion wherever it rears its ugly mismatched head.

"Dear Lord, Dick," Tracy coos into his wristwatch, eyelashes fluttering. "It's almost Christmas and that woman on the corner is wearing white tennis shoes and black stockings. Horrible."

"Not only that," Dick responds. "Look at those ghastly gold chains hanging from her neck. Something must be done. Get her!"

I guess that's a little rude. Truth is, Tracy is a scratch golfer (I never broke a hundred) and Dick's handyman skills (no pun intended) would make that obnoxious guy on *This Old House* green with envy. Besides me and Deirdre, they're the most compatible lovers Liam has ever known. Day after day, Tracy goes to the Green Lantern Country Club where–weather permitting–he hustles a couple of suckers on the golf course, often pocketing three or four hundred bucks for a couple hours work. In winter, he shakes down those same suckers at the card table, assuring them he just learned how to play that *particular* type of poker week before last. When his workday is through he comes to Rainbow Street, drinks Cape Cods at the end of the bar, and reads the *Rocky Mountain News* from front to back. Every single word, every single day. He and Dick discuss the stories in the paper, imagining themselves in the same scenarios as the victims in the Metro section, then they quiz each other on what they would do if they found themselves in a similar predicament. Tracy calls the game, "If-the-Loser was-You."

"Okay, honey, here we go," Tracy says to Dick, pointing with his cocktail. "If-the-Loser-was-You. Let's say you're a sporting goods storeowner and a customer comes in just before closing. He's got dirty blonde hair pulled into a ponytail and blue eyes that make you quiver. Very handsome–in a rugged, unshaven-Brad-Pitt kind of way–and he says he'd like to stay after the store has closed because he *really* wants to buy those Solomon skis and his sister has gone home for the money. 'By the way,' he whispers as he touches your arm. 'You're kind of cute.' Okay loser, what do you do?" Tracy asks, taking a slug of his Cape Cod. "Come on, time is running out. He's waiting."

"Are you kidding me?" Dick answers as he dries a mug with

his musty bar towel. "Brad-Pitt rugged? I let him stay and we see just how rugged he can be."

"Sorry, sweetie," Tracy says, pointing to the newspaper. "You lose. It says here that he lets his gang of thugs in and they tie you to a treadmill with a jump rope. Then they beat you silly, steal your wallet and your pants and all the cash in the register, before they shoot you in the head and disappear into the dark. Good night," he concludes, tilting his head from side to side with finality.

"Would you two queers shut the hell up," Bart Morris grumbles, shifting his bloodshot eyes from the television behind the bar. "Don't you two ever get sick of talking? Jesus, every day it's the same, 'What if you were on that 747 that crashed?' 'Imagine your grand-mother goes ballistic with an Uzi.' Christ, it'd drive anybody nuts."

"Oh Bartholomew, you love our little games," Tracy counters. "You're just a homophobe, that's all. We understand. Really, we do. If your mother allowed you to play with Barbies when you were young, you'd be much more in touch with your feminine side, much more secure in your sexuality. We forgive you."

"Christ, shut up with your talk. Enough already. You're giving me a fuckin' headache. Hey Dick, tell yer buddy to close it. And turn up the television, would ya? I'd rather listen to Vitale than this shit."

Yes, a late December night in Rainbow Street South. Dick and Tracy discuss the tragedies of the day, Bartholomew Morris bit-terly bemoans his plight, and the assembled regulars drink their drinks and smoke their smokes. Paper snowflakes twist on strings attached to the ceiling, red and green holiday garlands hang from the bar, and the illuminated beer signs in the window blink on and off, their ordinary messages augmented by the Christmas lights hung unevenly about them. Silverware scrapes against porcelain plates, a drunken couple argues at the door, and Burl Ives croons "Jingle Bells" from the jukebox. The smell of burnt beans wafts through the air. And my brother Liam, a spectator to this nightly parade, writes in his notebook and studies it all from his perch near the window–detached, alone, safe. He'd much rather watch than participate. That's what writers and scholars do, you know–they sit near windows, they watch.

At a cluster of tables in the back corner, the attendants from

Perpetual Journey Retirement Home enjoy their Christmas party, telling stories about the invalids in their care. Liam watches them from afar, amazed that they act and speak as if Death isn't waiting outside for them too.

"Yeah," one overweight nurse says, setting her margarita on the table. "If Mr. Potter was eighteen years old, I'd have him arrested, but he's eighty-five and knows he can get away with anything. He's like an octopus, that guy. Grabbing my ass, reaching for my tits, the guy's insatiable. Then he looks at me with those Marty Feldman eyes, licking his lips, and I can't help but laugh at the old letch."

The nurses at the table laugh and nod and flip ashes from their cigarettes into the half-filled plastic ashtray.

"Well, what about Mrs. Ogden?" another nurse asks, blowing her cigarette smoke into the air. "The woman simply refuses to wear any underwear and, let me tell you, the stench that comes from under that nightgown would make a mongrel run and hide. Hm, hm, hm."

Yes, some folks–like Dick-Tracy, Mr. Morris, the nurses, and others–live unexamined lives. My brother Liam, however, sits at a window table in Rainbow Street South *over* examining the hell out of his own. "What if I'd have been there?" he thinks. "How did it feel when the blood filled his lungs? Why us again?" The Murphy's creamy on his tongue, the carpenter's pencil clutched tightly in his hand, Liam furrows his brow and writes and drinks and wonders. Then he drops the pencil in defeat, removes his glasses, rubs his eyes, and curses under his breath.

"May 16th. That fuckin' day. The last day of our lives, Seanny. The last day for all of us."

Then, as so often happens when he's finished the fourth or fifth pint of the night, Liam floats back to that fateful day in May, the day that tore both of us from our old lives forever. For me it was a day of beauty and surprise and loss, for Liam it was a day for Napoleon and the sun. But hell, I'll let him tell you about it, he's more of the life-of-the-mind type than me. Like I said, I'm no scholar.

By the way, I'm Sean, Liam's older brother, and no matter how much I disagree with all of Liam's philosophizing and over examining, no matter how different the two of us are, I guess I have no room to criticize. After all, it's my fault he drinks here alone night after night, listening to the banter of Bart and Dick-Tracy, hiding from the uncertain world outside Rainbow Street's windows. Truth is, if I wouldn't have been such a clumsy ass last May, Liam wouldn't be so fucked up in the head right now. Hell, you don't have to be a Senecus or a Titicus to realize that. Yeah, I'm no brainiac, but even *I* know it's my death that's killing him.

. . . the young man who composedly periled his life and lost it has done exceedingly well for himself, while the man who has not periled his life and retains it to old age in riches has perhaps achieved nothing for himself worth mentioning.

—Walt Whitman

The Death of Little Napoleon
by
Liam McGarrity

Behind St. Cecilia's Church (where Billy Radcliffe saw a vision of a black Virgin Mary in 1981), across the street from Tryon Municipal Hospital (where my mom died in 1988), stands the Tryon Inn, the sole watering hole in my hometown of Tryon, California. At the TI, faded pool tables stand in dark, dusty corners, dated, sentimental pop songs play on an obsolete jukebox, and a dozen barely-employed drunks sit atop cracked vinyl bar stools smoking like chimneys. Last May 15th, Benny, Stanley, and I stayed a little late at that fine establishment, singing songs from the 80's, assuring ourselves we were handsome, fit, and special, so the next morning when my alarm went off at seven-thirty I pressed the snooze and slept fitfully until eight. I was hung over, wounded again.

The familiar sun-faded drapes of my childhood were the first things to greet my weary eyes. I knew everything that could be known about the NFL names on those curtains because, after my mom died, I would hide in that small room for fear my dad would accuse me of a crime I did not commit or a deficiency I could not remedy. His nightly drinking bouts (Sean said he single-handedly kept Jameson afloat) usually resulted in a barrage of insults, accusations, and broken bottles. When he was in that state, I would retreat to my room, lock the door, and lay on the bed, playing word games with the names on those NFL curtains. So I knew that the Rams were from Mars, the Jets were a jest, and there was a monster from Arizona named Slanidrac. In that room, I read Sean's stolen books, listened to his Doors records, concocted anagrams from familiar words; did *anything* to distract myself from the blubbering Irish idiot in the kitchen. The idiot who asked my sisters, Nora and Molly, questions to which nobody had the answers. Questions like, "Why?" and, "Why me?"

My father no longer asked unanswerable questions, but last May 16th he occupied the same wooden chair in the kitchen. When I walked in, he wheeled quickly in his seat to greet me. Since he'd been sober for five years (much to their chagrin, Jameson had to thrive without his ample support), he was annoyingly alert in the mornings. As so often happened, the first thing from his mouth was a cliché he'd learned in his Upper Glanmire schoolhouse.

"Ya can't hoot with the owls and expect to roise with the chickens, Liam," he chirped. "Morning always comes airly."

Turning my back to him, I nodded and filled the kettle for tea. My dad was headless beneath a whirling blue cloud of smoke. The periodic slurping of coffee, a rustling of a newspaper, or an emphysemic wheeze was the only evidence of his presence. He'd probably been up since five, drinking his two pots of coffee, reading the paper, smoking his cigarettes, sending up a hazy pall of smoke throughout the house. He was often lost in a blue cloud of smoke, a disembodied voice spouting maxims in a thick Irish brogue.

"Son, know this," he once said to me when I asked him why he smoked so much. "A man's got to have *some* vaices, he *needs* them for Chrissake. And since I've given up the bottle (God help me, I haven't had a Jameson in years) the smook is the only vaice left me. If I lived any cleaner I'd be a bloody Prod, for Chrissake. And if I was a Prod, I wouldn't live at all. Not at all."

While he continued smoking, rustling, and slurping, I sat on the kitchen counter and looked through the kitchen window to the dense morning fog outside.

"We gonna be able to get out?" I asked, stirring my tea. "It looks pretty thick out there."

"Well, son, says here," he quickly replied, pointing to the paper like it was gospel, "the marine layer will burn off around noon and

THE DAZZLE OF THE LIGHT

it'll go up to haighty later. Usual gray–May business. You look and see nothin' but clouds, no clue the sun is there at all, like; then, before you know it, there she is, baking your skin. We'll get out…we'll see fine. That's if you get off your lazy ass, of course. I'd like to hit some balls before we tee off. Get movin'."

Through the smoke and the unspoken grievances between us, I drank my tea and spoke to him of the L.A. Kings and the golf day ahead, anything to bridge the chasm. Then I rose, showered, dressed, and went to the garage to load our golf clubs into the bed of my pickup. My dad closed the garage door after me, stomped out his cigarette on the driveway, and got into the truck. I walked to the driver's side door and–because I was dressed only in shorts and a cotton T-shirt–shivered with an unseasonable chill.

The thick Pacific mist fell on my hair, face, and clothes, it eerily pressed down upon the foothills, the orange groves, the entire Tryon landscape. A strange silence accompanied it, a hushed anticipation, like the fog was the inaudible precursor of a drama as yet untold. Standing outside the driver's door, I looked skyward for a hint what that drama might be, but the sky was inscrutable, the sun nowhere to be found. So I climbed into the truck, fired the ignition, and shifted into reverse. I couldn't help but think of things hidden behind clouds and smoke, things far beyond our petty instruments of apprehension, things separated by miles, years, or days. Then, as I put on the windshield wipers and drove toward the 55 freeway, I thought of brothers, fathers, and suns.

* * *

My brother Sean rose in Temecula–a town near the high desert of California–at five-thirty with the alarm. There were no clouds or marine layers outside his trailer, only the cool desert air rolling in from Baker and the sun over the foothills rising from God knows where. He turned to Deirdre, waking her with the weight of his arm across her stomach. She sleepily put her arm on his as he scratched her stomach lightly. Their eyes were still closed but sleep had softly relinquished its hold on them. She turned to him and they kissed, then made love in the gold and purple predawn morning. Quietly, being careful not to let their daughters Erin and Brigid hear;

slowly, being sure not to disturb the cocoon the night had secretly woven about them. They didn't say a word but their bodies spoke loudly, in a parlance only the flesh understands.

There was no television in the twenty-eight-foot trailer they'd parked in the campground at Sad Shepherd Lake. The AM-FM radio and the unnamed noises in the peopleless landscape were the only audible intrusions besides the speech of the four. Sad Shepherd was a campground and fishing hole designed for the weekend vacationer. The one-and-a-half armed ranger, Frank Paloma, let Sean, Deirdre, and the kids stay free of charge because Sean said:

"Frank, we're building a house on some land I bought out near Joseph Landing. It's a great spot. Lake Elsinore in the distance, the Santa Ana Mountains nestled behind. Eden, Frank, another fuckin' Eden. It'll be like no other when it's done, but I need a little more time to get some cash together right now. The lot was pricier than I anticipated." Then he put his hand on Frank's shoulder like they were longtime friends. "But hey, let me show you what I've got planned…"

Frank listened to the story of Sean's dream, watching his eyes dance as he excitedly made some sketches on a worn legal pad. Sean described where the windows would go and what would be seen through them; he told him what type of grass would grow in the front yard and the games the children would play upon it; he sketched an upstairs den and spoke of the solace that would come to him there. And because he had the gift of gab, Frank saw the house come alive as if it already existed somewhere besides Sean's imagination. Frank told Sean he could stay at Sad Shepherd as long as he needed, provided he worked a few shifts in the front booth taking money and giving directions. They came to an understanding because each man recognized something of himself in the other. Each fancied himself a rebel, a man who does things other people conceive of in the dead of night or in the throes of a dreamy stupor, but doesn't have the courage to do under the watchful gaze of the sun.

As Sean and the girls ate their breakfasts they spoke quietly, almost in whispers, because there was nothing to speak above and therefore no reason to raise their voices. After eating, they each went to their chores eager to start the day. Sean tended the dog outside and his visible breath gave witness to the chill. Brigid and Erin made their beds and got ready for school and play, never once thinking that it might be the last day of their childhood. Deirdre went to wash the dishes and make the bed in which she and Sean made love. She smiled as she stood over the sink, thinking of mornings, thinking of days.

Before departing, Sean kissed each of them in turn, touching their faces with his cracked carpenter's hands, looking into their eyes on release. Deirdre grabbed his left hand and kissed the line where the doctors had reattached his thumb after a Skilsaw accident. She said, "Be careful, be careful." Sean nodded and walked out the door. Banshee, his yellow lab, anxiously waited in the back of his Ford pickup, like she was a leader or guide taking him to a place only she and a few others knew about. Her tail wagged, her mouth hung open, and her ribs shone gold through her coat.

Together they drove away from the trailer and Banshee wagged her tail and Sean held his coffee mug away from him, trying not to spill as he bounced over the unpaved road. The dust spread behind the Ford in a vee and settled like powdered cocoa on the leaves and the water behind them. The sun was red and then orange and on the same level as the truck and Sean squinted then reached for the sunglasses on the dash to cover his deep-set eyes. The steam from his coffee wafted murkily in the sunlight and dampened the middle of the windshield as it tried to escape upward. Sean hummed along with the Hothouse Flowers on the stereo as they sang about breath appearing as steam on a winter's morning. He pet Banshee's head as she poked it through the sliding window behind his bench seat. Then he sang to her like a lover and she licked his face, whimpering in his ear all the while.

"There is so much to breathe, see, know, understand, and do," Sean creakily sang in his best Irish accent. "I believe in tings of beauty. . . Do you? *Do you?*"

From the trailer, Deirdre and the girls heard Sean's voice, the muffled music at high volume, and Banshee's bark as a chorus. The voices and music grew fainter and fainter as Sean's truck progressed farther and farther down the road. Eventually, the woman and her daughters were left alone in the silence with no idea what the day might bring, no inkling what the day might take.

* * *

When my first practice shot on the driving range somehow flew from the heel of my driver directly between my legs and into the calcium-deficient ankle of the elderly woman golfing next to me, it became clear that I would not become a PGA-caliber player in the thirty minutes before tee time. The woman dropped to the ground, whimpering pathetically. A crowd quickly gathered, a few duffers gave me disparaging glances like I injured her on purpose, and my dad walked away, trying to create some distance between himself and his embarrassing son. After the woman stopped crying, her husband wrote down my name and address and assured me I would receive a bill from their doctor. The crowd dispersed, looking reproachfully over their shoulders like I was some kind of sadist who enjoyed hobbling brittle-boned old women. The woman walked away gingerly, using her three-wood and two-iron as makeshift crutches, and I was left alone, seething and embarrassed.

Golfers, like campers, are permitted to drink at any hour of the day, so I walked to the cantina to get a beer, hoping that the alcohol would ease my frustration. A platinum-blonde cantina worker turned to fill my order and I waited impatiently, thinking about Little Napoleon–my nemesis, my defining trait, my ego incarnate. All the McGarritys have one, though I didn't hear mine until the day my mother died. That's when the Frenchman started whispering in my ear. He convinced me that in payment for my mother's departure to the spiritual world, my success in the physical world was somehow guaranteed. So on that August day twelve years ago, Little Napoleon began to harden me to this world, saying:

"Mon frere, c'est tout. You've taken your medicine like a man. Zat's all zair is now. Because of zis, you are stronger zan ze others and tout le monde will pay for your pain. Tout le monde. You've paid ze price, monsieur, maintenant, ze world is yours. La morte cannot touch you now. Show zat bitch what one angry man can do."

Little Napoleon has only gotten louder since. He resembles his namesake, Napoleon Bonaparte, in every way: bellicose, domineering, willful, unyielding, obsessed with victory, iron of will, and because of some injustice suffered as a child, a giant chip on his shoulder. The historians would have you believe that Napoleon died of stomach cancer in 1821 on the island of St. Helena, but I knew, as I sat on the low brick wall beside the cantina drinking my beer, that the bastard pulsed in my blood, spurring me to subdue things that no mortal has ever subdued. Because of him, I raged, because of him, I thought the world owed me something, because of him I thought golf with my dad and brother-in-law on a Tuesday morning was as important as the Battle of the Nile. Because of him, I believed that through simple force of will I could control what happened in my life.

But as the red emergency van sped into the parking lot (sirens blazing), and they loaded the whimpering old woman that I'd injured into the back, I was beginning to doubt the wisdom of Little Napoleon's counsel. Something told me that he and I were both deluded.

I shook my head and looked at the sky. Far above my petty battles and concerns, the sun began to peek pink through the coastal mist. In the five minutes it took to finish my beer the mist and the clouds had gone and the sun began to brazenly dry the sweat on my forehead. I cursed the sun without looking at it because I knew the day would be a hot one and I couldn't do a thing to prevent it. Then I looked to the ground beneath me and felt the earth's substantial weight, its cool permanence. I was caught between the dense ground under my feet and the dissipating sky and its cruel master above. I sensed something bigger beyond my paltry world waiting, but cowered in fear lest it come.

Many suns rose on many shores and I was too small to see them. Many blades of grass were bent under many winds and I hadn't given them a thought. I'd never once read Walt Whitman.

* * *

My massive brother-in-law, Charlie, shook me from my reflections of Little Napoleon and the sun with a hearty slap on the back. He handed me another beer and said, "You ready?"

My dad limped toward us off the range, the sweat pouring relentlessly from his brow.

"Jaysus, Mary, and Joseph, we've *been* reddee, man," he bellowed. "Once again, you're behind the times like the back of a clock, Charlie. Glad you could finally make it."

Charlie looked at me and smiled, ignoring my father's verbal blast. "What's with the fossil?" he asked as we walked to the first tee. "Little Napoleon out early today or what?"

"Yeah," I said. "Unfortunately, he's out in both of us. What are you gonna do? It is what it is."

"Great," Charlie responded. "Should be a fun day."

Because Little Napoleon convinced me I was the center of the universe, I was certain that the twenty or so people loitering in front of the clubhouse, putting on the practice green, and lounging in the pro shop, were staring at me as I pulled the driver from my bag. So with the imagined eyes of a multitude fixed squarely on my person, I teed the ball up, felt the weight on my front foot, swung nice and easy, and landed safely down the middle of the fairway a little over two hundred yards away. Acting casual, I sauntered back to the cart with the tee in my mouth like I expected nothing less, then collapsed into the seat with relief.

Charlie was next up at the tee. With a voice like thunder and a body as big as Wisconsin, subtlety is not his strong suit. Charlie's a man of contradictions–an artistic salesman, an intelligent buffoon, a pagan Christian. Years before, when he'd graduated from a conservative Christian college in Placentia, Charlie made a deal with Jesus Christ that–as far as I can gather from his lifestyle and political viewpoints–went something like this:

"Though I plan on living a life of the flesh *now*, Lord, I promise to come back to you at the end. Yes, I realize that the world of the flesh is a temporary one, a pale show, but eternity will have to wait. I want cavernous cars, sleek boats, rare steaks, and a beautiful wife with whom to share them. I want a taste of this American Dream they all talk about. In my defense, as you remember, I lived on a commune in Utah for fourteen years so you have to admit that I deserve a break now. I'll check in occasionally–Easter, Christmas, etc.–and I'll familiarize my children with the tenets of the Bible, but a man's gotta live, doesn't he? Darn right. Forgive me Jesus, but you yourself said that we know not what we do. So let's make a deal. I *pretend* I'm a Christian now, giving voice to the doctrines, arguing with the agnostics, etc., and you give me a moment before I die to actually become one. Bottom line, I don't want to rot in hell. I'm on your side, you know? So, we got a deal? Great, great, good to hear it. Amen then, talk to ya later, big guy."

Charlie's face is sun-weathered and wide, his arms mottled and massive, and though he plays basketball and all other sports about as gracefully as a Sumo wrestler, there's one thing for certain: he can hit a golf ball a friggin' mile. Looking at his titanium-shafted driver admiringly (like it was a metal child he'd fathered), he took two practice swings, the velocity of which created a small weather system behind him. Then he teed his ball up, crushed a drive about twenty yards shy of the green, and yelled (like he was talking about someone else), "YOU DA MAN!" Then he dropped his club behind him and followed the ball a few steps down the fairway. I cringed at this breach of golf etiquette and shook my head, because he's just a good-natured lout with more girth and heart than sense.

Then there's the old man. My father wears his wrinkles much like a tree wears its weathered bark. As proof of his durability, the things he'd outlasted and therefore beaten. His faded jeans were baggy in the back and hung low off his hips. He hitched them higher with his gnarled hand as he teed up the ball. The back of his neck was wrinkled like old leather and I thought how amazing it was that he'd worked outside for fifty years and his Irish skin was fair and his head was bald and he'd had only one case of skin cancer and it was benign. Indestructible, stubborn, tough as nails. Funny, if I took after my mom's side of the family I'd be dead before I was forty-five. If I took after my dad's side I'd live to be eighty, but I'd be crazier than a loon. If I split the middle and took after both sides of the family, I'd die a fifty-eight-year-old drunken cancer patient running for the Ward Spokesperson position at the local insane asylum. Boy, I can't wait for the future.

My father's arms were much smaller than they were when I was younger, the skin loose with spidery veins running through them, but that's what time does to the best of us. He was also a couple of inches shorter than he used to be and I wanted to tell him, "Dad, you're growing down like a cow's tail," one of his favorite adages, but it seemed natural that he was smaller than he'd been because I think that's what life should do to you. Time and its defeats, petty slights, and injustices, should chisel away at your physical stature, then the years pass and Time should chip away at your pride, ego, vanity, the remnants falling like so many ponderous shavings from your essence, and as you watch the waste fall all around you, you should finally understand how paltry and transient this world of flesh really is. You should understand how vulnerable you are, no matter what happened in the past, no matter what dictator is living in your chest.

But when my dad got off that boat in 1957, the chisels of Time had not yet fashioned him thus. In '57, he was wide-eyed, confident in his young strapping body, unshakable in the belief that, in America, a hard-working man with a good head on his shoulders was immune to the defeatist demeanor of those pathetic old men in Ireland who told him he'd be back before year's end. So after a beautiful oceanic voyage and a brief sojourn in Canada, he moved to Buffalo and found a South Buffalo lass of Irish ancestry. They married and he worked building houses and they had children and he worked and they moved to California and he worked and she made the home and taught the children and he worked and she cleaned and cooked and he worked some more. They bought a home, purchased brand new automobiles, enjoyed small victories, all in the encompassing California sun. With each swing of his 28-ounce Vaughan hammer he grew larger, arms extending long enough to wrap around one, two, three, then four children, Time's chisels impervious to his massive frame.

But, much to his chagrin, my dad didn't leave death behind in the grass, pubs, and potatoes of Ireland, as the advertisers of the shipping line whose vessel carried him here wanted him to believe. So his wife was sick (tink, tink, tink, Time's hammer pounding on the chisel head) then dead (the assumption of invincibility falling at his feet) and there was nobody to pay the bills, to cook for the kids, to pop him the first beer of the day. Thus, on a day in August of 1988, he began to shrink because Time and its chisels went to work on him relentlessly. He felt tricked. So he drank and worked and screamed her name in the middle of the night, but still he worked some more and never missed a day for any reason. The years went by and we all left the house and one day, five years ago, he looked in the mirror at his yellow eyes and bloated stomach that he couldn't touch for the tenderness of his liver. He hated what Time had done to him, but he still wanted to live, so he stopped drinking that day and hasn't had a drop since.

As he stood over that golf ball he was smaller, true, weaker in body, maybe, but he was also sober and golfing with his son, probably thinking that the hard part was behind him. Nothing but the green grass of Mesa Verde Golf Course, green pastures ahead.

He swung at his ball and Charlie giggled like a schoolgirl behind him because he thinks my dad swinging a golf club looks like a lumberjack chopping down a tree. The ball looked good in the air–straight, long, dead center–but my dad said, "Oh no," because he thinks that if he expects bad things to happen it safeguards him from them actually occurring, but if they *do* he's anticipated them so the blow isn't nearly as devastating. Backwards, I know, but it's the Irish way.

Charlie yelled, "TIMBER!" and I thought of Time and its chisels, the sun and the smoke, what it means to be Irish, and the fact that a dictator lived in my bosom. Then I pressed the accelerator on the cart and smiled a bittersweet smile. We were off, carrying our golf clubs and all the other things that men carry with them as they feebly inch their way through their sometimes imperious, sometimes beautiful, but always foudroyant, fleeting lives.

* * *

As he walked into Rancho California Lumber, Sean nodded at the clerks and felt the heavy stares of the red-vested managers who knew the status of his account. Jill and Cheryl, the solicitous, bovine women at the cash registers, smiled at him and said good morning. He returned their greeting in kind and walked to the back of the store to where the commercial accounts were handled. There stood Jackie–one of the five or six black people within a thirty-mile radius of Temecula–with his thick arms at rest on the counter, his head bent forward as he filled out the invoice before him. Jackie looked up when he heard Sean sing:

"Little ditty, 'bout Jack and Di-aaa-ANN...Two young Americans doin' best they can, HUH!"

Jackie shook his head, smiling down on the paper, and said,

"Damn, Sean, my wife's name *still* ain't Diane and you *still* can't get the words to that song right. Even after all this time."

"The words to a song don't matter," Sean said as he leaned on the counter. "You know that, Jack. What's important is that a man wants to sing. That's all that counts."

"Maybe, you're right, Sean," Jackie said, shaking his head from side to side. "Maybe you're right."

"How're things goin' with that lovely wife of yours anyway?" Sean asked.

"Ah, you know, all right, gettin' by, gettin' by, I guess," Jackie responded. "But things *can't* be going well for you. Carl says I can't give you any more lumber on credit without you giving me some earnest money first. You owe him. Big time."

Sean looked down at his yellow boots, smiled, and said, "I know that Jackie, but put yourself in my situation. I'm a small contractor who doesn't get paid until I finish the job. I can't finish the job unless I have the lumber. That's called the workingman's Catch-22. I'm damned if I do and damned if I don't. But listen, I just need ten more sheets of half-inch ply and I can finish sheeting the roof and that cheap bastard I'm building for will give me *some* money, at least. Come on Jackie, you know I'm good for it."

Sean flashed that grin which had kept him out of so many other jams: the dimples, the tan wrinkles around the blue-burning eyes. Jackie smiled back at him because he knew there was a kernel of truth nestled somewhere in the bullshit Sean was slinging. He knew he was dealing with an honest con man.

"Sean, I don't know nothing about catching a 22, but I, personally, got no problem wit you. Me and you are cool, I'm just a working man, too. But if I give you that lumber, Carl's gonna have my black ass strung up. Can't do it."

Accepting the inevitable, Sean said, "All right, Jackie, all right, I'll cut you a check. How much cash is it gonna take to convince that bloodsuckin' German boss of yours that I'm earnest?"

"He needs at least five."

"Five it is," Sean replied as he pulled out his checkbook.

Shielding the negative balance from Jackie with his left hand, Sean penned the check with his right. As he did so, he thought what a bastard Carl–the owner of Rancho California Lumber–was for his parsimonious, begrudging nature. *The poor bastard*, Sean thought as he shook his head, *he thinks that money has anything to do with anything.* Sean smiled as he signed his name because he'd created yet another financial difficulty for the McGarrity clan. He wondered what Deirdre would say about another bounced check, thinking of the abuse he'd suffer for not valuing a dollar as much as others. But he wrote the check anyway because he needed the lumber right then and he'd figure out what to do about the deficit later. Some would call that irresponsible but Sean called it appreciating the importance of the moment in which he was living. Unlike Carl, Sean refused to live his life miles and years from where he stood.

He handed Jackie the check and Jackie called to the yard for his order. They high-fived each other and spoke of the Lakers and the beauty of Kobe Bryant's high-flying dunk of the night before. Only they called the move sweet, not beautiful, because they were working men who were afraid to be called wimps and only wimps use fancy words like that. Sean told Jackie that he taught Kobe that move and that he was going to learn the words to that song if it killed him. Jackie said, "Keep singing brother, keep singing."

As he walked through the store to the lumberyard out back, loud enough for Jackie to hear, Sean yelled, "SUCKIN' ON CHILI-DOGS, OUTSIDE THE TASTEE FREE-EAZE. DIANE SITTIN' ON JACKIE'S LAP, HE'S GOT HIS HANDS BETWEEN HER KNEES–HUH!"

With his back to the counter Sean raised a backwards wave to Jackie. The outline of his form punctured the sunlight in the door like the ethereal silhouette of some otherworldly creature only come to pay a visit. Jackie smiled as he watched him go and sang the chorus of their song to himself. The chorus that said something about life going on long after the thrill of living is gone. As he totaled up the invoice from Sean's order, Jackie thought that was true for Carl and most of the rest of us, but not all, no, it's certainly not true for everybody. He thought how some people are thrilled right to the end. Jackie still heard Sean singing as he walked into the yard to load his plywood. He held Sean's bad check in his left hand and decided to hide it in the back of the drawer for a few days, give him a chance to make some money in the meantime.

"What the hell," Jackie whispered to himself. "The working men gotta catch a 22 together. Fuck Carl. I don't owe *him* a goddamn thing."

* * *

As my nine-iron hurtled through the air toward the water hazard to the left of the eighteenth green, I thought of Harry Macklin, a teacher and coach at the old alma mater, Tryon High.

Harry Macklin was more like an anti-football coach than an actual football coach. A diminutive pacifist who dabbled in Eastern philosophy, Coach Macklin spoke to us of things far beyond our Tryon High practice fields. As he gazed whimsically into the Tryon Hills with a spear of grass in his mouth, he would speak of the *Upanishads*, the *Bhagavad Gita*, and the Ganges with the ease and assurance of an eastern mystic. One day, after a particularly difficult loss, he compared our team to the Harijans in India, the untouchables destined to endure poverty, sickness, and squalor. We were bad that season (one win, ten losses), but bad together and Coach Macklin said that's what being a family or an untouchable is all about: you've got to play the hand life dealt you, got to stick with those who share your defeat. He said there was something ennobling about loss, something enduring in the lessons of travail. Since none of us really knew what ennobling or travail meant, we just stared at him blankly. We didn't know what the hell he was talking about. A few years later, Coach Macklin was fired for his football teams' perennial ineptitude. Apparently the school board didn't see the poignancy of a football coach well versed in the teachings of Gandhi, nor did they understand that perhaps the most important lesson we can learn in this life is how to accept the most difficult of losses.

But as my nine-iron flew through the air–glistening in the sun, making helicopter noises–and splashed into the pond, disappearing with a gurgle, I realized that I hadn't learned one thing from Coach Macklin. Why couldn't I accept the fact that I couldn't golf well? Why couldn't I accept that my brother-in-law cheats every time we play? Why couldn't I accept loss? Why the hell couldn't I accept that things were beyond my control?

Overall, I shot a 118, which–for those of you unfamiliar with golf–was about as well as Napoleon did at Waterloo. Needless to say, both Little Napoleon and I thought our inept golf display was the end of the world, the single most significant thing happening anywhere on the globe. We were pissed. When the little bastard's in that state, my only recourse is to sedate him with alcohol, tranquilize him into submission. So as my dad, Charlie, and I sat in the clubhouse after the round watching golf on television, I drank more Budweisers and pouted, wishing that Little Napoleon would go away forever, wishing I could let go of things that were already lost.

But it's useless to wish for the impossible, some things simply aren't meant to be. If I was truly one of Coach Macklin's untouchables, I would've realized that things just *are*, most essential things remain fundamentally unchanged: people drink, cheat, curse, reach, fall, and die; the sun comes, rises, torments, hides, shines, and sinks. As I watched the sun through the clubhouse windows–inhaling the smoke from my dad's umpteenth cigarette, listening to Charlie's salesman babble–I should've known that things remained as they'd been before we started, as they'd been forever and will remain forever still.

And a hundred Napoleons and a truckload of beers couldn't change that.

* * *

Mike Trademan was the sole employee of Sean's company, Temecula Valley Builders, but 'employee' might not be the right word because he didn't get paid with any degree of regularity and TVB wasn't much of a company. A post office box, some business cards, a few rudimentary sketches, and a contractor's license number on file in Sacramento, was the only tangible evidence of its existence.

Mike and I had been friends since we were eight years old. We played football together in a youth league for Judge Rocker, a man who thought that kids in America had it too easy. The Judge thought that the affluence of the post-World War II years, together with those damn hippies and sexually-liberated weirdos, had created a society of cholesterol-clogged, video-addicted, sedentary children who needed someone to teach them discipline, dedication, diet, and what it means to be a *real* man. He thought he was just the guy for the job. Unlike Coach Macklin, the Judge probably couldn't even find India on a map, let alone expound on its philosophies. His interests didn't venture beyond the life and times of George S. Patton, the California adventures of Richard Nixon, and the history of the National Football League.

About five years after I played for him, the Judge married Sean and Deirdre on a cliff overlooking Laguna Beach and the Pacific. There were shards of white sun on each of the waves, splintering with the rise of the swells, blinding with the sweep of the sun. The waves kept coming and coming against the cliff without cease, without mercy, the repetitive crash a reminder nobody heeded. As Sean's best man, I stood at his elbow watching the Judge as he spoke to the gathering, periodically turning to the surf below the point, wondering how the Judge could be so close to those waves and the ocean life yet remain so oblivious.

Two lovers walked hand in hand along the shore, tossing bits of fish to the seagulls whirling noisily above them. A naked toddler waddled after a sand crab that had burrowed into the earth, the ring of the crab's circular entry point glistening golden and silver in the wet sand. And about a hundred yards or so offshore, what appeared to be a bouquet of wilted flowers floated between the waves. The waterlogged flowers rose to the crest of one wave and then slid down the back, awaiting the next wave's approach. I wondered if they were discarded by an earlier bride or maybe thrown to the sea by a widower bidding the ashes of his wife farewell.

One after the other the waves came, carrying the flowers, beating the cliffs down, smoothing the rocks below, calling to the people who walked by their liquid demise, but no one listening. The waves were simply emissaries of Time and its relentlessness, allies both of renewal and destruction, and it struck me that all the people at the wedding, including the Judge, were like those flowers out there in the jagged surf. We too were caught between the swelling and cresting waves, in a world that seems foreign at one moment, exciting and perilous the next, but always fatal in the end. People live because it's all they know to do, but the earth seems like a chaotic sea at times, like we simply don't belong here at all. We're like the fragile aging petals of a desperate flower; a flower that belongs rooted on dry ground but is plucked and thrown by some invisible hand to the sea instead. Because it has only known life, the flower fights to survive in the water, it tries to be unafraid of the bigger waves as they approach to carry it to the shore, but it somehow intuits that survival is impossible. It knows that one wave will eventually throw its lifeless form onto the sand. Some people, like the Judge, want to change the color of the sea, the inevitability of its cycles, or the frequency at which the waves plangently beg at the shore. Personally, I'm just hoping for a beautiful beach on which to alight.

But I'm getting sidetracked a bit. When Sean arrived late at the work site last May 16th, it's certain that neither Judge Rocker, Richard Nixon, nor the Harijans were in his thoughts. The completion of the roof, however, was. Sean and Mike sat on the down tailgate of the white Ford pickup and talked about the work before them, like if they described it in enough detail and pictured it clearly enough in their minds, it would somehow get done on its own. Banshee ran to and fro, retrieving the rag bone Sean threw for her, inhaling the remnants of a sugar donut Mike was kind enough to give her. They each found pleasure in the morning sun, the sultry desert air, the anticipation of a day spent outdoors.

They eventually started their work but Sean was different and it's hard to say exactly how. Usually he was as dynamic as a sparrow that knows that if he stops the beating of his frail wings, eventually he'll fall to the ground. He'd run from one side of the house to the other, jog to the edge of the roof to retrieve a level, eat a ham and mustard sandwich on the run, always competing in a race between himself and an invisible foe. Constant movement was his trademark. It was like he knew that if he stopped just once, he'd stop forever. And every day he would challenge the status quo, the world-as-is, beating his smiling face against uncaring walls, trying to devour that which was withheld, explaining his dreams to men who had lost the capacity to fashion their own. But this world usually tries to break the spirit of such men, often killing those who won't change, succumb, or accept incomplete offerings. Men like Sean are destined to fall very early in life, but it's for the best, because the saddest thing in the world is a broken old man whose fallen in love with his defeat, though only so he can pity himself afterward.

So on May 16th Sean was not his usual self, but then again he could've been his perfect self, I'm not really sure. What I do know is that a calmness overcame him, a certainty and nonchalance that belied a change within him; a secret to which only a stranger was privy. He worked at an even, steady pace, like he was tired but still lucid, like he'd exhausted all his energy and in his depletion had found the rhythm he worked all his life to find. As it turned out, the rhythm found him.

So he and Mike went to work and Sean was not as frantic or frenzied as normal, not as animated as his usual self. He did not jump in the air, jabbing and talking like Ali, he did not race with Banshee through the dirt, did not sing any of his favorite songs. He methodically and fluidly pounded the nails and cut his cuts. He measured once and every estimate was correct. He pulled the sheets of ply to the roof, covering the framing with the wood that would protect a family he would never know. As he worked, the tools became extensions of his hands, the house a part of his body. An uncharacteristic calmness settled on his shoulders. He was poised as he worked, certain of his step.

That's why when he fell from the roof the first time it was such a surprise to him. The right heel slipped backwards, the left foot followed, and he was over the edge and down. As he fell it was like he was outside himself, a spectator watching the actions of another. And then he landed on the ground with a thump, checked his limbs to ensure they were intact, cursed himself, and wiped the chalky dust from his back and shorts as he rose. Mike pointed and laughed, slapped his knee, then laughed some more. Sean shook his head and climbed the ladder to begin again. As his face became even with the roof he looked to the ground and Banshee wagging her tail below him. Again, he shook his head, either in awe or disbelief, like he remembered something he'd forgotten, like it was more than ten feet to the ground.

At the edge of the roof, the same circular saw that years before had severed his thumb at the knuckle, lay prone, like a wounded animal in the sun. Deirdre told me Sean was calm the day he severed his thumb, too. She screamed and said, "Oh my God!" and he told her to relax and call for the ambulance. Only a thin layer of skin held his thumb to the rest of him, but after a mad dash to the hospital they were able to save it. Afterwards, it looked like he was always giving a crooked thumbs-up. Deirdre told me he looked at the saw that day–blood gushing from his hand all the while–like it was a family dog who'd betrayed its master by biting the hand that brought the proverbial food. He took offense that the tool he'd shined, serviced, cared for so tenderly had treated him so maliciously in return. I guess the last thing this world needs is a sensitive carpenter, a man who treats his tools like family and his appendages like loans from a neighborhood pawn shop.

The same saw that had once betrayed him glinted in the sun and Sean accepted it back into his hand like a cuckold reluctantly accepting his unfaithful lover's comforting caress. The plywood sheets he'd acquired by nefarious means at Rancho California Lumber rested half on the roof, half off, in a temporary support he'd built for that purpose. He pulled a sheet from the pile and measured and marked it with the carpenter's pencil that had his teeth marks on its sides. The saw cut the air then the wood with its efficient scream and the scrap pieces and the sawdust fell yellow and disconsolate at his feet. The healing smell of cut lumber was pungent in his nose and the sawdust made him want to sneeze, so he looked at the sun to force the issue and lost his balance once more. His work boots failed him, the sun blinded him, and he slipped and fell off the roof again.

As Mike once again laughed at his clumsiness and pointed to his prostrate form, Sean saw the roof looming above him: the yellow wood, the skeletal framing, the outline of a virgin chimney. Banshee ran to his side and licked his cheek, as if reassuring him of something, and Sean became suddenly frightened because it felt like some one or thing was doing this to him. It was like he was an animate puppet who just realized he had no control over his movements, gestures, destiny. But at the same time the fall *was* his destiny and a moment of utter lucidity overwhelmed him and, for the first time ever, he remembered that he'd been falling his whole life: from undependable motorcycles, off of home-made skateboards, from unbroken horses as they bucked. This was the latest in a series of falls that began when he was a boy and Sean somehow saw he had to fall. And like all men who see Truth, who understand that they are at the service of a will larger than their own, he became scared because it suddenly dawned on him that what he wanted mattered not one whit. What he wished and willed had absolutely no effect on the way things were.

But the fear he felt–that there was a will stronger than his own, belonging to some unknowable puppeteer out in the beyond somewhere–is the last fear there is to face. As he lay on his back there, the dirt warm on his skin, his dog Banshee beside him, Sean seemed to finally understand. In that split second he saw that a man who does not fear the hand that pushes him, or the other hand that waits to catch him when he's done here, is a man who is eternal. Death can't touch the man who knows no fear, but it rips the heart out of the man who defies it, the man who fights it at every turn and thinks he's stronger than everything, like Napoleon.

He let the puppeteer decide what to do next.

Sean laughed nervously in response to Mike's ridicule and after a brief moment his fear subsided, like the dissipating mist of the marine layer to the inevitable heat of the sun. He picked himself up, like he'd done so many times before, and walked to the ladder. Banshee nipped his hand playfully and he touched her snout one last time. A certainty came to him as he walked and he ascended the ladder forgivingly, blinking long and slow as he rose. He was curious to see what awaited him on the roof and the ladder was the only avenue open, the only choice the puppeteer made available for him to find out. The aluminum ladder creaked with his weight and delivered him upward to his destiny.

When he arrived on the roof he slowly turned in circles, as if he wanted to remember this world one last time. The Santa Ana Mountains to the west, his siblings and father beyond them; Sad Shepherd Lake to the south, Deirdre, Erin, and Brigid laughing at play on its shores; and in the great unseen Elsewhere, the unvisited countries, the unsailed seas, the unscaled mountains calling to his adventurous soul. All of it was out there. And it might have been the circles, it might have been the sawdust at the edge of the roof, it might have been the blinding sun above, and it might have been that puppeteer nobody's ever seen, but *something* caused the last fall.

That's right, still a third time he fell and this time his fall was broken by the temporary support he'd built below him, but it wasn't temporary at all, it turned out to be the most permanent thing there was. It held and stayed and he was bent backwards over it as he fell to the ground. His neck buckled backwards and he was almost impaled. His body crashed to the ground and he groaned. He lay there crumpled, like some twisted beginning, a gnarled man looking down an abandoned road nobody else can even see. His legs were slightly spread, his arms above his head with the palms up in a gesture of supplication, and if I had been the sun looking down on him that day, he would have looked like a broken letter Y in repose.

Banshee ran to his side and whimpered.

Mike heard Sean and the dog and rushed to their side. Banshee screamed like, well, you know, like one of her namesakes wailing for the coming of the dead. She looked to the sky and barked, yelling at something or someone unseen by human eyes. She cried and cried and Mike yelled at her to be quiet because the pitch of her voice confirmed what he felt in his heart: that some things are unchangeable, that facts can't be replaced by our feeble hopes for a different tomorrow.

"Shut the fuck up, Banshee," Mike yelled. "I'm trying to think here. Are you all right, Sean? Say something for Chrissake."

Sean gasped for the breaths that became shorter and shorter. Mike ran to the house on the hill above to call the paramedics. The white-haired woman who answered the door made him wipe his dusty work boots on the porch mat that read "Welcome." He wanted to strike her but couldn't spare the time.

Sean's breaths grew shorter still.

The sun wasn't breathing at all.

When Mike returned he saw Sean's prostrate form and his broken sunglasses at his side. Sean's eyes reflected the liquid blue of the sky and the mesmerizing yellow of the sun and he choked on something within him. His chest heaved but still he wouldn't look away, he refused to blink or turn his gaze from the sun. So he lay there on his back, his bronze chest wide, bare, unprotected in the yellow sun, his blue eyes dazzling in anticipation of something that none of us squarely planted on this side can ever fully know.

And he smiled.

Mike grabbed his hand and Sean lightly clasped his in return as if none of it made any difference, as if gestures held no meaning. Mike told him he'd be all right although he heard Banshee still keening beside him and didn't quite believe it himself. The dog and he both knew that Sean was dying and there was nothing to be done by either. Sean's breath was shallow, the blood filling up his lungs, chasing the air away until there was no room for the air at all. Mike again told Sean he'd be all right. Sean stared straight above, still unblinking, and managed to whisper:

"I *know* I'm going to be all right . . . I'm going to die . . ."

And as he took the last breath in his lungs his eyes grew wide in a greeting to something I've never seen. And with all that was left of the end of his time, he uttered a commonplace epithet and then invited his invisible conqueror with one simple word; a word that doubled as a legacy and seemed to say it all.

He screamed, "C'MON."

With her snout turned skyward, Banshee howled–almost keened–at the sun, like whatever she had seen had taken her master there. And at twenty-nine years old, my brother, Sean McGarrity, was dead. Like so many before him, he would remain forever young.

* * *

Meanwhile, the sun reflected off the chrome bumper of the Volkswagen in front of me as my dad and I sat in late-afternoon traffic on the 405 freeway. We were just south of John Wayne Airport inching our way to my sister Nora's house for dinner. It was a bright white flash like a giant photographer's bulb bursting in my eyes and simultaneously capturing a still moment on earth. I turned my eyes away. Things all over the world were happening and I couldn't know what they were. I couldn't stop them or change them even if I did. It was useless to fight.

A teenaged surfer studied the sets of waves near 38th Street as they broke methodically on the sand at his feet, his bathing suit damp from the morning session. A brown-skinned woman turned over on her stomach to sun her back at Newport and watched the surfer, her breasts cold beneath her wet top and soft as velvet. A man in Anaheim poured himself a cup of coffee, trying to shake off the afternoon lethargy, and the crumbs of the nondairy creamer made him think of a childhood lover he'd lost. A secretary in San Clemente touched herself under her desk thinking of the man who signed her checks, wishing that a thrill might invigorate her otherwise monotonous life. The Judge sat on his bench at the courthouse in Santa Ana and sentenced a man to thirty years in prison because (besides his skin color being too dark) he had too many strikes against him. Speaking of black people, Jackie couldn't get Sean's song out of his head and he cursed him and spun like Kobe Bryant around a pallet of two-by-fours, then he dunked a foam coffee cup in a dumpster and thought about thrills, old songs, young women in jeans. My friend, Benny, read Richard Brautigan under a tree in his backyard, thinking about Big Sur and Kenneth Patchen, wondering what it'd be like to watch whales at sunset while sipping a Chardonnay. In Santa Margarita, Nora peppered the salad then suckled Melinda, her three-month-old infant, never once thinking about death and white flashes. My other sister, Molly, sat at her desk at UCLA devising ways to attack a two-three zone. My dad sat quietly beside me fighting off his nap (wondering why he never called his brother in Ireland to tell him all the things brothers tell each other), and I cursed the morons like me who sit in their cars on the 405 and think that it's living.

And in the instant that the sun bounced off that bumper all the cosmic tumblers clicked into place. I hid my eyes because it was too much to see, too much to accept. It was a flash of omniscience, a piercing of the veil of time and space that I could not allow. I looked away while the sun proudly hung over all of our lives, mocking our blindness with its distorting charm. The white burst from that bumper was the sun telling me that it was stronger than I; that it knew millions of things I would never know. It ogled all of us from above—Sean, my dad, Molly, Nora, Deirdre, the kids—like it was a petty god in an extinct religion and we were the supplicants who'd forgotten to pray. The sun held all the world's mysterious dramas in its gaze and I was too weak to face them, too blinded by its reflection to see.

But now I know that the secret the sun kept hidden in its bosom, the promise it held in its stoic heart, was that Little Napoleon and my brother lay dead together in the dirt of Temecula a hundred miles to the east. Ignorant of the magnitude of that passing instant,

I drove down the 405 freeway with Budweisers and Nora's twice-baked potatoes on my mind, never once wondering about puppeteers and the falls they effect, dead brothers and the company they keep, or destiny and the tyrants who fight it.

So now, a year-and-a-half later, I sit in this North Denver bar drinking yet another pint of Murphy's, replaying the sixteenth of last May over and over again. The saturnine morning, the treacherous lumber, the dispassionate sun a silent witness to a murder. While I study the past–arguing questions of fate and free will–the present days pass by this bar's window, forever irretrievable, forever lost.

But I can't concern myself with that world right now. You see, my brother Sean is dead. And I can't get over it.

TWO

The good news is that I didn't have to deal with that Kraut, Carl, about that bad check I wrote at Rancho California Lumber. (Hell, if I would've known I was gonna die that day I would've screwed him for even more material.) Of course the bad news is that my girls and family are lost to me now forever. At least in the flesh. I don't want to get too ethereal or sound like that femme-boy Patrick Swayze in *Ghost*, but suffice to say, what's lost to the flesh is multiplied in the spirit. A million fold. So I can't physically touch them anymore, that's true, but what I get in return is more than fair recompense. Trust me. As for the living, in time their loss will be transformed into something beautiful, something lasting. Like the old man once said, "Son, the flutes that make the sweetest music are whittled with the sharpest knives."

Which brings me back to Liam. The kid can make some beautiful music with that pencil of his (actually the pencil's mine), but his real life, the one outside the margins of that notebook, is in the crapper. And no matter what kind of bullshit he slings about Little Napoleon dying with me, don't believe it. Little Napoleon's the one poisoning Liam's mind with talk that self-preservation is paramount. He's the one selling Liam on the idea that it's better to stay inside and write than it is to go outside and live. With the help of Dick-Tracy, Walt Whitman, Rebecca Kelly, and a few others, I hope to convince the kid otherwise.

"Another?" Dick asks as he picks up Liam's glass and wipes the table. "Tracy says he's buying."

"You know me, Dick. I'd drink turpentine if somebody else

41

bought it for me. Thanks, Tracy."

"My pleasure, dear sir," Tracy calls from the bar. "The only payment I require is a recitation of a poem from our good gay poet, if you please. Something with young males frolicking in the surf, if at all possible."

"Sure, Tracy. Least I could do."

So Liam sets his pencil and notebook down, flips through his copy of *Leaves of Grass*, and pauses at the inscription on the title page. In large cursive writing, it reads:

Liam,
Thought you could use this. Scratch that. I <u>know</u> you can use it.
Rebecca

Liam shakes his head to dislodge the image of Rebecca Kelly from his mind. Rebecca, his beautiful co-worker at Big Bob's Market, Rebecca, the woman who haunts his mind daily. Then he finds a suitable passage and begins to read. Dick delivers his pint and returns to his post behind the bar. Like a sonorous foghorn, Leonard Cohen's voice seeps from the house speakers, singing of Suzanne and tea and honey.

"From pent-up aching rivers..." Liam begins.

Tracy closes his eyes and mumbles, "Yes...pent-up...aching..."

"...From my own voice resonant, singing the phallus..."

"Yes, Walt, sing of the phallus, play that skin flute."

"...singing the muscular urge and the blending,/Singing the bedfellow's song..."

Tracy says, "Liam, any more of this and I'm going to have to take Dick into the kitchen and give him the business. Talk about aching phalluses."

Hearing the poetry come alive, Tracy holds his fresh Cape Cod and imagines the salt air thick in his nostrils (he's never actually been to the ocean), the sun warm on his bronze, muscular shoulders (they're neither bronze nor muscular), and dozens of swimmers at play in the surf. Dick throws a towel over his shoulder, leans on the bar, and looks to the ceiling, imagining his own personal paradise: a gaggle of twenty-year-old men bathing him in a monstrous mountain hot tub, laughing and caressing, praising and cajoling.

"Touch me," Liam continues. "Touch the palm of your hand to my body as I pass, be not afraid of my body."

Grumbling, Bart Morris rises from his barstool and says, "Christ, I'm going to the can. If it's not faggot bartenders serving me scotch, it's faggot poets ruining my nights. Thanks, Liam, I'd expect more from you. I thought you were a hetero."

Liam looks up from the pages, but before he can respond a gregarious regular named Rudolph Jordan strides through the door and bellows, "Of course he's a hetero, Morris, he's just a non-practicing one at the moment."

Rudolph winks at Liam, raises his arms high over his head, and shouts his usual greeting.

"Friends, Romans, countrymen, lend me your beers! I do not come to praise Anheuser-Busch, I come to bury him. Right square in the graveyard of my liver. Line 'em up, Dickey boy, line 'em up!"

The entire bar turns to watch him approach.

"Hello all, hello! Bring on the Budweisers, Dickey, a man is no camel!" he concludes as he hangs his coat by the door.

"Close the damn door, Rudolph," Dick yells from behind the bar. "Not everybody is as hot-blooded as you."

The regulars wave and hallo him. Rudolph nods and smiles, pats a few old friends on the shoulders, points at a few of the nurses at the party in the back. Slowly he makes his way to the bar to pick up the two pints of Bud Light Dick has already poured for him.

"Liam, my dear friend!" Rudolph booms as he walks toward his table. "How's it hanging, Shakespeare, how's it hanging?" he asks, setting his beers down gruffly while pulling up a chair that had not been offered. A piece of bloodstained toilet paper protrudes from his left nostril, evidence of his inevitable afternoon nosebleed. His face is blotchy, crimson and blue, like that of an overweight fighter who's been pummeled for fifty rounds or so. Before continuing, he downs one pint in a single, wide-mouthed gulp.

"What ya writing?" he asks after a mighty belch, pointing to Liam's notebook then wiping the sweat-stained strands of blond hair from his forehead. "Not some more stuff about carpenters dyin', I hope. Cheesus Criminy, that crap depresses me," he says with disgust. "Why don't you write some stories that people *want* to read, like a mystery or somethin'. A little intrigue."

He shifts his chair closer to Liam's and says in a conspiratorial tone, "Now that Tom Clancy, *he* can spin a yarn. Dean Koontz too, he scares the bejesus out of me. But John Grisham's the master, boy, he can keep you guessing for hours. Did he do it? Didn't he do it? The suspense slays me. Yep, nothing like a good courtroom drama to get the blood boiling. That stuff *you* write about bores me to no end, Liam. You gotta jazz it up a little bit," he says, snapping his fingers like he's keeping beat to some unheard tune. "You gotta write about some babes, some gangsters, some terrorists or something. Give the people what they want, Liam. Trust me when I tell you that *no*body wants to read about the depressing shit *you* write about."

This insightful analyst of the contemporary publishing scene smells of stale alcohol and fetid sweat, but you have no choice but to love him. He's got a Charlie-Brown face, vacant brown eyes, and a purple birthmark the shape of Texas on his left forearm that he can't help from scratching over and over again. It's like he's certain the blemish will eventually come off, he's just gotta keep picking at it.

"Let him be, Mr. Jordan," Tracy calls from the bar. "Our young friend here is interested in the intricacies of the shot, not whether he birdies the hole or not. And certainly not whether the gallery gets a thrill. Unlike you and me, *he's* not playing for an audience."

"What the hell are you talking about, pillow biter?" Rudolph asks. "I'm talking about writing and you're talking about golf. Get a clue, fancy pants, and mind your own damn business."

"I'm trying, my dear overweight friend, to put Liam's situation into terms you can understand. Sports terms, that is."

"Was I talkin' to you, Tracy? Did I pull up a chair near you? Did I ask to drink next to you? Oh, I must be confused, I thought I was sitting at *Liam's* table, discussing *Liam's* stories."

"Rudolph," Liam interrupts. "Do you think I *want* to write about this stuff? I've told you before, I *have* to, I have no choice. I'm *compelled* by things beyond my control, Rudolph; do you get it? Do you understand?" he begs, exasperated. "Christ, I feel haunted by it, like Sean's standing right next to me and I've got to accept his death in prose before he'll go away."

But the words fail to penetrate Rudolph's very thick skull. With a blank expression, he stares at Liam and says:

"Hey, all's I'm saying is that I don't see anybody with a gun to your head, Liam. I'm just telling you what people want to read. They sure as hell don't want to be reminded they might die in a friggin' accident, man, *that* I know for certain. You might as well write about the Holocaust or the Hindenburg, for Chrissake. All I'm saying is if you want to make a buck or two, if you want to see your book on the shelf next to *real* writers like Sidney Sheldon and Clive Cussler, you gotta change your approach. Don't bite my head off, I'm just trying to help you out."

Rudolph lifts his second pint of beer and closes his eyes, his pink tongue puncturing a beatific smile as the glass approaches his lips. He takes half the glass in one mighty draught. Then he lifts his arms, shrugs, and says, "Hey man, I'm your friend, I'm just givin' it to you straight. Dick, turn up Sportscenter would ya?" he yells across the bar, wiping the foam of the cold beer from his lips. "I had fifty on the Nuggets today. Gotta see how they did."

"Drink up, Rudolph," Dick says as he points the remote control at the television, the volume rising. "The Christmas party starts soon and you're nowhere close to being ready."

"Yeah, yeah," Rudolph responds. "I'll be ready, you just keep pouring, pal, don't worry about me."

While Rudolph and Dick speak across the bar to one another about the sports of the day and the imminent holiday party, Liam crinkles his eyes, confused by his present state. *How?* he wonders, sweeping the bar with his gaze. *How in the hell has it come to this? I used to have my shit together, but now I hide here, act-ing like a little sunlight will kill me.*

It's true, Liam *has* changed. He used to be a man possessed. After Mom died, he lived with a vengeance, rising above the oth-ers. Man, it was beautiful; the kid was cocky as a jaybird. In high school, he quarterbacked his team to respectability, earned a GPA a shade under 3.9, and won a scholarship to West Texas State University where he was named All-Mountain Conference twice and an Academic All-American once. Women, fellow students, and teammates were inexorably drawn to him, his assuredness almost palpable in his wake. He was certain that nothing could harm him further so he strode through the world like a titan. Out of college, he was drafted by the Denver Broncos, where only a future-Hall of Famer named Elway could keep him out of the lineup. I was proud as hell. While playing for the Broncos he attended law school at night because he knew his football career would end, but the need for relentless attorneys never would. He and Little Napoleon were on the rise, astounding teachers, coaches, and family with a zeal and audacity that virtually guaranteed success. Like Liam himself said, he lived with a chip on his shoulder and the chip served him very well.

Until last May 16th, that is, that was when the shit hit the fan. Yeah, that day Liam realized that the ladder he'd been using to climb to the peaks of his athletic, academic, and material worlds, the ladder Little Napoleon told him was so sound and sure, was really made out of straw. And that realization was the spark that consumed that ladder in flames. Poof. Gone. Smoke, ashes, heartache. And as Liam looked at the remnants of his former life burning around him, his face smeared with soot, his clothes ragged and charred like one of those old cartoons, he realized that Mom's death did not buy him immunity like Little Napoleon made him believe. So I wasn't the only member of the McGarrity clan to fall that spring day, Liam also crashed to the ground, killing a self that had existed for the ten-plus years since Mom's passing.

So in September, after being released by the Broncos (quarterbacks must have confidence and Liam now has none), and dropping out of University of Denver Law School (after all, my death couldn't be beaten in court, so what's the point?), Liam retreated to the obscurity of a small Denver guest house, a menial job, and this funereal bar a thousand miles from our home. He is afraid and damaged, vulnerable and alone. Once a strapping 200-pounder with steel blue eyes, raven black hair, and a swagger that would make Joe Namath proud, Liam now finds himself a scared, 170-pound store clerk who fears the light of day. The kid's a wreck, he really is.

"Okay boys," Rudolph wails as he downs yet another lager. "Line up, I think we're about ready. Come on, come on, gather round, don't be shy. It'll take about eight of you to do me justice, you little shites. Dick…maestro…the appropriate music please, let's get this Christmas party started." Then, rising from his chair and obscenely thrusting his massive hips, Rudolph repeats, "Let's get this party started!"

Liam looks around, uneasy, like he knows something is desperately amiss but he has no idea what. But Dick, Tracy, and the others have no such qualms; they all come when Rudolph beckons. Rudolph begins to stretch and perform toe-touches, knocking his chair backwards with a crash. He then quickly drains the glass of eggnog that Tracy has handed him, rubs his nose abrasively, and asks:

"How's the schnozz, everyone? She bright enough for ya yet?"

The others scream, their eyes glassy with drink, their faces glistening with laughter. All the patrons–drinks in their hands–encircle Rudolph. Even Bart Morris cracks a smile. Dick walks to the jukebox to program some songs. A nurse claps her hands in anticipation.

"My dear Rudolph, come on, it's only once a year, have another nog," Tracy implores, spilling his drink as he's bustled from behind by an intertwined couple. Rudolph complies, inhaling it quickly, his face dripping with sweat, his nose on fire with drink. And it suddenly dawns on Liam what is about to transpire.

Rudolph's given name is Lujah Charles Jordan, but he only answers to Rudolph now. A few years ago Tracy dubbed him Rudolph because when he's been drinking for an afternoon, his nose lights up like that beloved reindeer's and they treat him special because of his deformity just like Santa and Rudolph's fair-weather reindeer friends. During the holiday season, Rudolph is expected to arrive at the bar no later than six in the evening so that by the time the eggnog and caroling starts, he's half in the bag and in full luminescent flower. The patrons then pick him up in their arms and carry him around the bar and he laughs with his glassy eyes and lit nose (like a light bulb) and they act like they're delivering presents to the world and he's their gluttonous leader. He lifts his monstrous cranium like the thick smoke in the bar is an arctic fogbank through which he's navigating.

Now, four of the bravest (or drunkest) men each grab one of Rudolph's appendages, groaning and straining with the weight.

"Come on, you wussies," Rudolph taunts, another glass of nog mysteriously appearing in his hand. "Pick me up. Higher, higher! How the hell is this nose going to light the way so close to the ground? Rudolph needs altitude to guide us all to a magical yuletide. Higher…Higher!"

A few of the female nurses from Perpetual Journey get underneath his massive stomach and push from below. He is now spread-eagled four feet off the ground, aglow with perspiration, his bulbous nose seeming to grow brighter indeed.

"Higher! Higher!" he implores. "What will all the children do if Rudolph doesn't come? And…" he whispers lowly to the blond nurse beneath him, "Rudolph really wants to come. See what you can do, sweetie."

The woman shrieks with laughter and punches Rudolph in his giant gut. As quickly as she runs from beneath her massive burden, another woman takes her place. Finally, with the help of six inebriated men and three courageous women, Rudolph is lifted aloft and carried around the bar as the first few bars of "Rudolph the Red-Nosed Reindeer" play loudly from the house speakers. The mob moves in circles, Rudolph lifts his nose in the air, and the entire collection of lost souls bellows the child's Christmas song with glee. They seem to commiserate with the alienation of the strange reindeer and they hope that they too will find something in their minds, bodies, and souls to give their life some meaning, something to help them belong. In the meantime, though, they're happy with their drinks, their fleeting friendships, and this large good-humored man they carry above them.

"And if you ever saw it," they sing in unison. "You would even say it glows. Like a light bulb!"

At the table by the window, Liam watches this spectacle unfold and he too can't help but hum along with the tune. Before it gets any more raucous, Liam decides to head home to take Banshee for a walk. So while the local inebriates make another loop with Rudolph, their voices rising in shouts and squeals, Liam finishes his stout, picks up his things, and walks to the door. With one hand on the doorknob, he turns to watch the others. Rudolph sticks his nose in the air, turns his head from side to side like he's a levitating dog searching for a treat, and sings, "…all of the other reindeers used to laugh and call him names...like Pinocchio...!" Dick and Tracy follow behind the mob, their arms around each other's shoulders like old war veterans celebrating some past victory. Weary nurses and orderlies in soiled white and khaki uniforms laugh and drink and carry Rudolph in circles through the bar, bumping into chairs, disrupting family dinners. Bart Morris reaches behind the bar and pours himself another scotch, thinking, "What the hell, Dick wouldn't begrudge me a little holiday cheer."

It is December 22nd and–though I don't want to admit it–I guess Dick Hackett is right. At Rainbow Street South, drinking can indeed make you colorful.

* * *

When Liam opens the door, the noise from the party pollutes the tranquil winter night. The arctic air blows frigidly in Liam's face, shocking him as he departs. So cold in Colorado this time of year, he notes, so bracing to feel that chill air fill up your lungs. The smell of pine needles wafts fresh in his nostrils, the sound of brittle snow crunches beneath his shoes. The stars hang low above him, precariously hung in the sky like an interwoven fabric of stoic sentinels periodically peeking from behind the swift-moving clouds. Liam feels like he is being watched. The frigid wind blows into his face and creeps down his back. He shudders with a chill.

"Brutal fuckin' wind, Seanny," he says aloud to me. "Remember what Mom used to say about the wind, bro? Remember?"

The whistle of the breeze through the pines, the wail of a distant car horn, and the bark of a nearby backyard mutt are the only noises he hears in response to his question. But I remember quite well, Liam, I remember quite well. He walks through the wind, down tree-lined Emerson, along Lafayette and its forlorn vacant lots, to Hyperion, where he rents the guesthouse behind the home of Bob Scallipari, his boss at Big Bob's Market. At home, he's greeted by the sound of claws scratching from behind his front door and the whelp of a dog in ecstasy when he turns the key.

"Raaaarrrt, raaaarrt, raaaarrrt!" Banshee bellows.

Upon opening the door, Liam is welcomed with two well-placed paws in the middle of his stomach, like Banshee is a diminutive dance partner that won't be refused. She wags her tail, licks Liam's palm, then runs to the sideboard where she retrieves a leash in her mouth. Liam attaches the leash to her collar, sniffles with the shock of the cold, rubs the phlegm from his nose, and walks backs outside.

"I know, girl," he says as they walk across the backyard. "I know. It's good to see you too." He pats her chest roughly and asks, "Where is he, Banshee? Where the hell can he be tonight? Huh girl?"

Banshee looks over her shoulder at him, mouth agape, then proceeds out the side gate with purpose. She raises her nose into the frigid air, like she smells some faraway scent, feels some distant presence, and breaks into a trot. Like Liam, her breath blows ghostly white in the Colorado darkness and she feels an undeniable need to cover distance, to feel aches in her legs and lungs, as some verification that she *does* exist, that her presence is a buoyant testament to something she can not see but always senses near. At first, Liam clumsily follows behind her, but soon he too finds a comfortable gait. Banshee extends her stride and pulls the leash and Liam runs faster, curious to see where she'll go. And, in this North Denver night, the two of them run beside the whining city busses and their wraith-like cargo, across the snow-encrusted lawns and their memories of past springs, then, gasping and wheezing, they run by the rusted cars and gray homes of the spiritless automatons whose unfulfilled dreams litter their minds and hearts like so much stultifying clutter.

Then, panting, longing, striding, the man and the dog run through darkened alleys, weed-filled vacant lots, and abandoned playgrounds filled with the ghosts of long-dead children. Whether they run to escape some spirit's haunting or to search for something lost, I'm not really sure, but in their hearts, legs, and minds, the dog and the man both feel an unquenchable desire to run and run and run.

So that's what my brother and my dog do. They run.

What do you think has become of the young and old men?
And what do you think has become of the women and children?
They are alive and well somewhere…

–Walt Whitman

Defenseless
by
Liam McGarrity

2:06 P.M.–Sunny, warm, the spring wind beginning to rise from the foothills as an elderly bald man and his son walk up the driveway of a house in a typical South Orange County neighborhood–white stucco, red Spanish tiles, manicured lawns, shiny foreign automobiles. A disheveled woman runs from an opened garage to meet them. She is crying. The man and his son do not yet know why.

"It's, it's…" Nora began, stuttering as she walked to greet my dad and me as we slammed the doors of my truck. I could hear her baby crying from somewhere inside the house.

"What is it, Nora, what's the matter?" I asked, grabbing one of her shoulders. Charlie appeared in the doorway leading to the living room, holding the baby and shaking his head slowly.

"It's, it's, it's…" Nora sputtered, wiping the moisture from beneath her nose.

"Oh no," my dad said, like when he hooked his drive at Mesa Verde.

"It's Shhh, Shhh, Shhh…" she stuttered, unable to catch her breath.

"Oh no, oh no," my dad said, his hand on her other shoulder. A broken human triangle.

"What the fuck is it, Nora. Tell us!" I screamed.

"Th-th-there's b-b-been an ac-ss-ss-ss," she breathed deeply and spat, "…an accident."

"Who is it, Nora?" I asked again. "Relax, hon. Deep breaths, deep breaths. Tell us who it is, sweetie."

"Shaw, Shaw, Seanny. It's Seanny!" she yelled, bursting further into tears and crouching down, as if the uttered name of her fallen brother had become the spoken emblem of all things insufferable.

"What happened to Sean, Nora?" I begged. "Is he okay? Tell us where he is, Nora. Calm down and tell us where the hell Sean is!"

"He's with Mom, he's with Mom, he's with Mom, he's with Mom!" she screamed.

"Oh no, oh no, oh no, oh no!" my dad responded.

The three of us collapsed to our knees in unison, grabbing each other's hands in an anemic attempt at comfort or prayer. My sister wept, my father chanted, "Oh no," and I leaned back in rage, trying to acclimate myself to the knowledge that would so shape my life from that day forward. I broke free and punched the driveway (breaking my pinky and ring fingers), and stormed into the backyard, knocking over two trashcans and three white plastic chairs along the way. I seethed, paced, snorted, like a rabid fighter whose been waiting all his life for a worthy opponent and, search though he might, can not find him still. If Sonny Liston would've materialized from the sky, I could've destroyed him. Joe Frazier? Larry Holmes? Please. Don't make me laugh. But none of those adversaries materialized, nobody whose destruction would salve my wound appeared. There was nothing in this world equal to my rage, nobody present to punish for this news. My enemy, Sean's death, was everywhere yet nowhere at all. An opponent as elusive as the wind that blew in my face, as omnipotent as the sun that browned my shoulders. And then, in a flash, it came to me:

The sun.

The sun's intensity could almost rival my own, the sun was a foe almost worthy of my wrath. I felt it on my sunburned neck, my freckled cheeks, and the tops of my bronze arms. I looked into the sky and there it was–faceless, apathetic, dominant, a victim worthy of my Vesuvian rage. Yes, the sun was as big as Sean's death and

I wanted to kill it. So I bellowed some incoherent screech at the top of my lungs, jumped in the air like a madman, and started swinging. I flailed and kicked, screamed and cried, I cursed and leapt, swung and tried, yet, yet…I didn't land a single punch. In response to my futile ranting, the sun, of course, said nothing. It did not move. And as I panted in that backyard, wiping the tears from my eyes, I realized that the sun was just like Sean's death–it too was undefeatable and enveloping. It too was spread over everything.

I wanted to kill, but there was nothing to murder. I wanted to scream, but no one could hear. Wanted to hide, but there was no-where to go. Yeah, I wanted to run from the mocking sun or destroy it with a punch, but the sun–like death–is indifferent and unassailable. The sun is vast and you can't outrun it. The sun is immense and doesn't really care.

* * *

3:11 P.M.–Warmer still, the wind outside kicking up in still greater gusts, while our protagonists have retired to the interior of 1018 Avenida Pico, the typical South Orange County house mentioned above. A man on a white couch holds a crying baby in his left arm and his hysterical wife in his right. The elderly bald man stands in the doorway of the slider that leads to the backyard, looking pensively off into the distance, his hands thrust deep into his pockets. The man's son leans on the counter with a telephone crouched in his ear. He holds a Budweiser in his left hand and a pencil in his right. The news is spreading.

While drinking a Budweiser I fielded and made telephone calls, contacting those who in turn would contact others who in turn would notify still others, ad infinitum. Within thirty minutes, the word had spread to hundreds of friends, family members, and peripheral acquaintances like a vocally transmitted cancer. Thousands of questions were asked and millions of fragmentary answers were offered, but none of us could quite believe Sean was dead. No justification could be offered, no explanation made any sense. He was the most vibrant of us, the most alive, and we each felt guilty that he was the one that had to be sacrificed. If someone like Sean can die this early, we thought, why not me tomorrow? Why not our children tonight?

But details were fleshed out, locations ascertained, directions written down on scraps of paper, and before I could finish my third Budweiser, my dad and I were back in my truck, heading over the Ortega Highway on our way to the once-bucolic town of Temecula. We reached the Santa Ana Pass and began our downward descent to Temecula on the other side of the range. Far below, beside Sad Shepherd Lake, about seventy-five giant wind turbines turned. White, stark, stoic, their fan-like appendages turned and swirled in the wind at a height of fifty, sometimes a hundred feet off the arid ground.

The turbines reminded me of balsa-wood airplanes I had as a child, the ones with working propellers that were wound with common rubber bands. I'd wind those propellers until they were taut, aim toward the sun, and release the small plane skyward. Usually, the fragile machine would nosedive to the ground, shattering and splintering upon impact, but sometimes, just for a moment or so, the plane would take flight, actually ascending, climbing upward, higher then higher until it was lost in the sun. After a few pregnant moments, it came to rest on the ground and I would run to retrieve it, thankful the gift I had offered the sun was so dutifully returned.

But in contrast, the propellers of those wind turbines had no chance for flight, no chance to uproot themselves and soar on the wind. No, they were planted in the ground, not whimsical enough for flight. What a shame, to be anchored to the ground while the wind tugs at you to fly. Then, suddenly, my truck lurched sideways and I realized that the same wind that blew the arms of those turbines—generating power to all the homes and wineries in the valley below—now toyed with my truck, pushing it across the narrow and slight road. I was as much at the mercy of the wind as the childhood planes that either violently crashed to the ground or found a way to take an ever-so-brief flight. I, too, was defenseless against it.

Then, as I watched those turbines and thought of those childhood planes, I suddenly remembered what my mom used to say about the wind. My God, how could I not think about this until now? How could I not remember what Mom said the wind was? So as I

drove down that one-lane road and watched those wind turbines, I
heard voices that had long been silenced, saw people that had long
been dead:

I awoke in the middle of one winter's evening to find Sean and
my mom sitting in front of the fire, laughing and telling stories. I
coughed to let them know I was there; they turned, and invited me
to join them. The fire licked my face and the reflection of the flames
illumined my cheeks as my mother held me on her lap, talking about
the drafts that used to howl through her childhood home in Buffalo.
The wind outside our own house howled at the top of the chimney,
sending the flames dancing to and fro. It seems that my grand-
mother told my mom and her siblings that the wind in the house, the
chilly breezes that blew through the cracks and windows of their
South Buffalo home, were just evidence that their dead father had
come back for a little visit.

"You see, boys, when you die, God doesn't take you to heaven
right away," Mom said. "No sir. He lets you take your time, become used to the idea of not having your arms and legs and all that
other heavy stuff that gets you in so much trouble. Plus, there's so
much in this world to explore, so much that people like us never get
to see while we're alive because the Rockefellers and the other
dirty Protestants keep us locked up in factories or chained to tool
belts. Yeah, we work and they travel. But we'll get the last laugh,
boys, just wait and see. They think they travel first class, but just
wait 'til you see what God's got in store for *us*."

Sitting on my mother's lap, listening to her story, I watched
Sean across the room. He smiled, a glow on his cheeks, like, even
though he was seventeen years old, he still believed every word
Mom said.

"Because when you die," she continued, her eyes growing wide
with wonder. "You get to fly to wherever you'd like. Liam, think of
it," she said, rubbing my stomach as she looked over my shoulder at
me. "You always wanted to go to Ireland to see where your father
and grandmother were born, right? Well, in a blink you'd go across
America and its fields, mountains, and lakes, across the Atlantic
and its whales, fishes, and mighty ships, to Ireland, and you'd know
your father's house like it was your own and you'd look at the
waving fields of barley and the stone fences and the white cottages

and you'd know that Ireland was your home too. What joy, boys, what joy it must be to feel it! And Sean, that mountain in Nepal you keep talking about, the one all those people start to climb but never seem to finish? Well, you won't have to climb that damn mountain after all; you could just skim up its side, weightless, free, like a joyful whisper kissing its top! How 'bout that? Yes sir, when you die you move quicker than a thought, faster than a sunbeam."

I smiled at the thought of it, imagining the island of my ancestor's birth, riding the waves of the North Atlantic as they crashed into West Ireland's rocky shore, gliding atop Lough Gill and absorbing its poetic musings. Sean smiled too, thinking about that mountain he always hoped to climb. Mom continued:

"But you see, when these spirits go from one place to the next—scurrying from continent to continent, flying with joy and ecstasy as they go—it's only natural they kick up a little breeze behind 'em. So," she concluded. "The wind is simply the dead flying away, boys, enjoying this world one last time. That's why you've got to remember that the stronger the wind, the more dead have been here for a little visit, the more miraculous things are being seen in the world."

I shrank in my mother's bosom, terrified that the breeze coming down the chimney and causing the flames to dance; might just be the dead coming back for me.

"Stop that now, Liam. Shush. We shouldn't be afraid of the wind, son, we shouldn't curse it when it blows too hard. No, on the contrary, we should close our eyes and let it caress us, no matter how cold it might blow, because the wind lets us remember all the people that have passed. It's just a reminder of how beautiful it'll be when we go. Yes, boys, the wind is a comfort to us all."

"What about the Rockefellers," I asked, gazing into the fire, still a little uneasy. "What about the people that have already seen everything there is to see in the world? Where do *they* fly when they die, Mom?"

"Don't you worry about them, Liam," she answered as she tucked her blanket around my feet. "They never paid any attention to people like us when they were here, so we shouldn't pay them any mind when they're gone. Let the bloody Protestants fend for themselves."

* * *

6:39 PM–Sunset. Liam McGarrity arrives at the home of a friend of his brother to find families, friends, and strangers surrounding Deirdre McGarrity, his recently widowed sister-in-law. Decisions are made, morgues telephoned, consolations offered, and it's decided to take the family back to Tryon, deal with the crisis there. Liam takes Deirdre with him because, as another black-haired, blue-eyed McGarrity, he's the closest thing to Sean still alive. They drive in silence back to the campground, Deirdre clutching Liam's hand all the while.

After three hours of drinking, talking, retelling the events of the day, we decided that Deirdre and the kids should go back to Tryon to stay at her parents' house, keep her close to the family. The well-wishers thought that getting her away from the silence, the wind, the trees, and the unnerving thoughts that sometimes accompany those humbling phenomena, would be the best thing for her. I'm not sure that Orange County and its congestion, pressed-shirt indifference to flesh, and rejection of what most makes us human–conflict, sorrow, bittersweet laughter–is the best place for anybody, but Deirdre had been rendered a child again and readily agreed to anything.

So we drove.

We sped along the freeways, skirted the small country lanes, and bumped over the unpaved road that finally led to Sad Shepherd Lake campgrounds. Frank Paloma, the one-and-a-half-armed park ranger Sean had befriended a year before, had lowered the flag on the front booth to half-mast, like a fellow soldier had fallen. He stood stiffly at the gate, his Chicago Cubs hat held stoically in his left hand, and waved us through the gate with his stubby right. The tears ran down his wind-chapped face in tiny silver streams. We slowly drove past him as he offered his salute. Through the window of my truck he looked like a weeping handicapped statue guarding a sacred camp to which only a limited number of revolutionaries had been granted admission. He was shaken because one of his own was gone.

Deirdre went inside the trailer to collect some clothes for her and the girls while I waited outside in the wind. It always blew a little rougher near their campground, the expanse of Sad Shepherd Lake always inviting more wind to come. Sean's white Ford had somehow come to rest in front of their trailer and I couldn't figure out how it had gotten there. I walked to it and peered over the edge of the bed, spying Banshee's empty bowl inside. I couldn't help but wonder where she was, what happened to her after Sean's fall. Then I climbed onto the bed and rummaged through the rest of the contents there: a plastic bag full of dog biscuits, a six-foot level, some orange extension cords, and a steel ladder were all that lay outside the locked toolbox. Except, that is, for the cooler that still held Sean's lunch. Although I wasn't hungry, I opened the cooler and smashed the ham and mustard sandwich into my mouth, taking half of it in one bite. Then I put the lunchbox under my arm and saw that the sliding windows to the cab were unlocked. I opened them and reached inside to unlock the driver's door.

Sean's twenty-eight-ounce Vaughan hammer lay on the seat in front. I picked it up and put it inside the cooler for myself, feeling the sweeping contours of the white wood handle, knowing that Sean did the same only hours before. Then, from the glove compartment, I grabbed an unsharpened carpenter's pencil that said 'Temecula Valley Builders' on its side. An unsharpened pencil with the name of a now defunct company on its side. It didn't even have an eraser on it.

"What a fuckin' waste," I whispered.

"Sorry for your loss," Frank called, startling me as he walked up to the campsite. I quickly put the pencil in my pocket and locked the now useless truck's doors. Though I knew it was rude, I couldn't take my eyes off of Frank's deformed right arm. While he spoke, I stared at his misshapen appendage like in his disfigurement some answer for injustice might be found.

"Oh, thanks, Frank," I said. "Appreciate it. Unbelievable, huh?"

He shook his head, taking a seat in one of the chairs beside the dead fire pit.

"It sure is. Un-fucking-believable. He was one of those guys. A guy that . . . a guy who . . . who . . ." he stammered, looking for words he did not know. "Ah shit. I don't know what I'm saying. You know what I mean, don't you? A guy who'd do anything for you, a guy who would …he would…he was just one of those guys, you know?"

He looked at me searchingly, gesturing lamely with his stub arm. Though I could not articulate it at that moment, I've spent a year trying to explain what Frank meant when he said, "One of those guys." The best I can do is this. It's as though there exists in the world a malleable, clandestine army of men and women who, if they could be gathered in one place, might fill a small college's football stadium. The army is so well concealed that the members themselves have no clue they belong and if you told them about it they would want to resign their seats. That, of course, is why they belong to this army: they refuse to submit their will to any outside authority, be it moral, spiritual, or physical. But this army could never be gathered in one place anyway, because they live on tempestuous coasts near Big Sur where the ocean's roar drowns out the pleading of the telephone's ring; they live in isolated mountain cabins on the outskirts of Cripple Creek, Colorado, where the fax cannot reach. A few, like Frank and Sean, live in places like Sad Shepherd Lake, dreaming in trailers of things that will never be.

We've all met members of this army and we all know that their mission is not the mission of a conventional army. Yes, they are in search of more territory, but the country they seek is in the mind and heart and it's difficult to measure the advance of the enemy in those places. Their conquests are by-products of how they live, neither planned beforehand nor celebrated afterwards. There are no maps in this war; there are no ranks in this army. There is only joy and the realization that no one material thing will help us in our search to capture it. The members of this army realize that joy is not a time waiting for us tomorrow, heaven is not a place that exists elsewhere. Joy is a way of keeping your eyes and ears open incessantly and actively because–though there will be some unpleasantness, some cancer, some murder, a few decapitations, etc.–crucifying beauty is all around us, waiting for those with courage enough to devour it. Their wide eyes say yes, amen, I will take it all as it comes at me and I won't be distracted by things as mundane as negative bank account balances or unpaid mortgages. I won't wonder what is coming tomorrow or next week because that is a signal that I do not trust the cosmos and I do. I do. I trust it all.

The members of this army all say "C'mon" in their own way.

But that night I didn't know anything about any army of rebels, so in response to Frank's stammering attempt to describe what kind of man Sean was, I simply said:

"Yeah, man, he was beautiful." Then I rose from my chair, pointed to Frank, and asked, "You want a beer?"

"Yeah, Liam, I could fuckin' use one."

I retrieved two cans of Coors from the small refrigerator inside Sean and Deirdre's trailer and held them against the swollen fingers of my left hand, hoping the chill would alleviate the throbbing. I then walked to the back bedroom and, with my good hand, knocked on the closed door.

"Deirdre, you okay, sweetie?" I asked.

"Yeah, Liam," she replied with a sniffle. "I'm just getting some things together for me and the girls. I don't really know what to pack. Nobody ever tells you that kind of shit."

"Just do your best, sweetie," I responded. "It's a funeral not a fashion show."

"Tell my mother that," she quickly added. "You know she'll say something about my shoes or my dress or some other bullshit."

I laughed on my side of the door and she forced a giggle on hers. We were both pleased to find something else to think about for a moment. Her mother seemed like an apt target.

"Yeah, I can hear her nasally voice now. 'Deirdre, where did you get those *horrible* heels? And those nylons, my God, they look like someone took a razor to 'em. Haven't you ever seen *Steel Magnolias*? Now *those* women had some style at *their* funerals. Now pull yourself together, this is the first public day of your single life. You want to make a good impression on the new pool of eligible bachelors, don't you?' "

"I know," she sniffled through a giggle, "she's quite a woman. Jesus, I hope she leaves me alone just this once. Just give me a few more minutes, Liam, maybe I can find something that will please her. I shouldn't be long."

"Take your time," I said. "We don't have to get anywhere. The kids will be asleep by the time we get back to Tryon."

Then I put my palm flat against the thin door, trying to communicate something through the wood I couldn't say in words. Unbeknownst to me–while we were morbidly joking about funeral ward-robes and overbearing mothers–Deirdre was holding her soiled bed sheets close to her face, trying to taste and smell the husband she'd made love to, then lost, only hours before.

I walked outside with the two Coors cold in my hand and threw one to Frank. We sat by the empty fire pit in front of the trailer, drinking Sean's Coors, thinking and talking about the wind, the sun, and all the other things against which we really have no defense. Though he was the uneducated son of an Italian immigrant and I was the son of an Irish carpenter, we both thought we knew a thing or two. We were gettin' philosophical.

"Man, how do you see any of it comin'?" Frank asked. "I had an uncle who immigrated to Jersey. My Aunt Carmen said it took him fifteen years to find a sponsor, raise the money, complete all the paperwork, and he finally made it. You know, the huddled masses? All that bullshit? Well, he's in Jersey six days, six fuckin' days, and bam, shot dead in an alley. Vendetta deal. The guy thought he was someone else. Mistaken fuckin' identity." Frank took a swig of beer, shook his head, and muttered, "No, Liam, there's no justice in this world. And if there's no justice in this world, I don't see how there'll be some in any other."

"Yeah," I responded. "I guess you just gotta be ready all the time. On guard, alert, like a fighter. There's always something out there looking to drop your ass for the count."

Frank concurred and then proceeded to recount the stories of all the tragic deaths he'd heard of, seen on television, or read about in the tabloids: bus crashes, accidental poisonings, chokings, drownings, bludgeonings, suicides–senseless deaths all. And while he mused philosophically about our arbitrary human condition, re-citing the morbid details of so many merciless ends, I swept the landscape with my gaze, hoping some hint or clue might be hidden there. And I realized that in the aftermath of this one tragic death, even the most commonplace objects had taken on mythical signifi-cance. Even the most ordinary things had become sublime.

In the distance, the Santa Ana Mountains rose hauntingly gray, silhouetted against the burnt orange of the late afternoon sky like a line of hunched prophets humming a wordless psalm. The wind blew across Sad Shepherd Lake in gusts of twenty miles per hour, rippling the small lake's surface, sending rows and rows of broken and dimpled waves across and away until they were lost in the distance forever. Beside the lake, the wind turbines turned and turned, silhouetted against the encroaching dark. A fisherman on the far shore continued to cast overhead, though the wind swiftly blew the lure back on to the sand at his feet time after time after time. Clumsy in his heavy down parka, the man reached back then awkwardly thrust the pole forward, as if believing the wind would abate at any moment, as if hoping this cast would somehow be different. Again and again he cast, again and again the wind rebuked him. However, the trees that encircled the lake–birch, willow, oak–had no such difficulty in their relationship to the elements. They leaned with the wind, bending, accepting, knowing that if they did not acquiesce their limbs would be ripped from them forever.

Looking at the burning red sky, the cold gray mountains, the white turbines, the obstinate fisherman, the blustery blue lake and the frothy white caps that dotted its impermanent surface, I was awe-struck, stunned by the mystery in all of it. Though Sean had been dead for six hours and there were millions of things against which I had no defense–somehow, the world was still beautiful.

"How'd you hear about it?" Frank asked, looking into the top of the gold can, then squinting off into the distance. "Where were ya, I mean."

Feeding the fundamental need we all have to recount where we were and what we did at the most crucial moments of our lives, I opened and clenched my swollen fist and began to tell Frank about my day. And though I knew it was rude, I couldn't help but stare at his misshapen appendage, this flipper-like arm that hung from his right side so helplessly. It protruded about twelve inches from his shoulder at a forty-five degree angle. It wasn't a stub arm, it actually had a working hand on the end of it, but it was like who-ever created it had forgotten to include the lower half. Impetuous craftsmanship had placed his hand where his elbow should have been. I wondered how in the heck, with that incomplete arm, he could fight the things each of us has to fight in this life? How could he defend himself from the assailants all of us must face?

After we talked about the events of the day and the ferocity of the wind, after we drank all of Sean's beers save one, Frank again shook my hand with his withered stump and went back to work in the booth. After he left, I stared dreamily out into the white caps of Sad Shepherd Lake, wondering about the sun, the wind, one-armed men, and how we're all just so goddamn defenseless. The metallic clang of the trailer door slamming startled me from my reverie. I retrieved the two bags from Deirdre and loaded them in the back of the truck. Then I put Sean's cooler and hammer beside them in the bed and stowed his unsharpened pencil in the glove compartment in the cab.

Deirdre and I drove down the dirt lane toward the paved road at its end. I looked in the rearview mirror and saw Sean's ghostfully-white pickup parked in front of the darkened trailer. I wanted to go back to the truck and start the engine, revive the life of it somehow. One useless truck parked beside an empty trailer, one dead body abandoned in a distant morgue. I thought maybe I'd go back to the trailer and get in Sean's one truck, find his one dog, Banshee, and drive to San Bernardino to sleep in the parking lot of one San Bernardino County Morgue so my one brother wouldn't be there alone. My desire was for everything to have something to go with it, for every person to have someone else, for all people and animals to have a purpose. I wanted everybody to at least stand a chance against the wind and the sun. But those were just wishes and I wasn't one of those guys yet.

Instead, I simply drove down the dirt path that my brother's truck had startled into airborne powdered cocoa just hours before. I looked out the closed window to my left. Darkness, Sad Shepherd Lake, the unknown beyond. An old oak tremored beside the lane with the inevitably ceaseless wind and I rolled down my window so I could feel the breeze on my face, maybe try to become one of those guys. I stuck my hand out the window, laughing as the speed-induced wind caressed my cheeks. I sped up and smiled still more, knowing that I might swallow a bug at any moment, but that's the risk you take when you put your head outside the machines, when you place yourself in the middle of the elements. The force of air on my face increased as the truck gained speed and it made me feel better that Sean wasn't that far away. I knew then that what my mother had said all those years ago was true. The dead are everywhere the wind blows.

* * *

Banshee? Well, Mike delivered her to a friend's house in Tryon until Deirdre could pick her up the next day. She lay in the doorway of a strange doghouse, an untouched bowl of food by her side. Until precisely 4:44 in the morning–the time when Sean would let her out to go to the bathroom–Banshee whimpered at the wind, wondering where in the hell he'd gone.

And I don't know what to say about that.

The Market

THREE

People with cash are deluded. They act like it's a badge of honor that they've never built anything with their hands, gotten a splinter, or ridden a city bus. But it's not their ignorance so much as it is their smugness that pisses me off. Like they've got it all figured out. I'd love to see a few of those pricks on their deathbeds and see how smug they are then. These high-end lawyers in their high-end German cars, these slacker dot-com wusses who've never *really* seen the sun, never *really* kissed a girl. All of them chafe my hide. They hire Mexican immigrants to cook their meals, pay uneducated secretaries to take their calls. Hell, they'd probably hire someone to wipe their ass for 'em if they could. It's like they're moving in an antiseptic bubble of privilege, protected by silk suits, white gloves, fine BMWs. They never mix with the common man, never get their flippin' hands dirty. Jesus, don't get me started.

Others–like Frank Paloma and all the boys at the bar last night, like me and my bro and the rest of our family–have no choice but to mix with the peasants of the world. Hell, we *are* the peasants of the world. That's why at 5:43 AM, after walking and feeding Banshee, Liam stands at the bus shelter on the corner of Hyperion and Rainbow. He shuffles his feet from side to side, tucks his chin into his coat, and blows into his hands to warm them. As the bus approaches, Liam retrieves *Leaves of Grass* from his armpit, inhales the diesel exhaust of the lurching bus, and waits to board. Climbing the stairs, he smiles at the warmth of the bus then shudders when he inhales the air inside. A heady mixture of body odor, patchouli, pine air-freshener, and cheap cologne hovers in the air. Yet despite the rank odors they emit, Liam feels completely at ease with his co-passengers, because no matter how much education and philosophy he gets, no matter how much he considers himself an "artiste," he knows he's still one of them. Just like me and my dad, just like Uncle Walt.

A homeless man lays on a seat in back, muttering a litany of unattainable wishes like a rosary-reciting nun; a mousy, Kafkaesque businessman notices a rip in his worn coat pocket and quickly covers it with his hand, hoping his boss will not see; a recent immigrant from Nicaragua watches anxiously as the foreign street signs pass, praying he'll recognize his stop when it approaches; a shy student with thick glasses reads a book of soft porn then sighs and closes the cover, knowing he has to return to the Tennyson his teacher has assigned; a red-caped woman with an unlit pipe in her mouth stares defiantly ahead of her, trying to hide the utter dread that flutters in her gut; a purple-haired punk-rock chick tongues the stud in her lip and shakes her head from side to side to the beat of the Bad Religion on her headphones. Mexican nannies with small children, homeless veterans with fingerless gloves, and nondescript laborers with dashed hopes, look out the windows as the bus pulls away from the curb, dreaming of a day that might never come.

"Merry Christmas, Liam," the slight bus driver, Isaac, says as Liam deposits his quarters. "Ho-ho-ho and all that other stuff."

"Mornin', Isaac," Liam replies. "But I wouldn't count your chickens, man, neither one of us has made it to Christmas yet."

"Damn, you do have a way of lookin' on the dark side, Liam. Things can't be as bad as all that. Can they?"

"Nah, Isaac, I'm all right," Liam says as he takes the bench seat behind him. "'Bout the same as yesterday anyway."

"Sorry to hear that," Isaac says. "If I remember correctly, you weren't doin' all that good yesterday. In fact, you kind of looked like shit, hanging a little bit."

"Thanks, man, I appreciate that," Liam says as he shakes the ice from his boots. "You know, it's an Irish thing. We curse the world and drink and the more we drink the more there is to curse at. Funny how that works."

"It sho' is," Isaac says as he checks his mirror and accelerates through the intersection. "It sho' is."

Mrs. Livingston (an elderly handicapped woman who rides the bus daily) smiles across the aisle at Liam. He smiles sheepishly in return. The bus rumbles past the early morning bakeries, the childless schools, and the faded brick houses, while the passengers look out the steamy windows, smile at acquaintances, or avoid the particularly distasteful. The diesel engine whines. Isaac leans toward the microphone to his left and says in his syrupy Lou Rawls voice, "Next stop, Camden Avenue. Camden Ave. is next."

Liam opens *Leaves of Grass* and begins to read. Ahh, the encompassing arms of Whitman. His words include every damn thing, completely at ease with Death, God, the sun, even all the misfits on this bus. Liam has often thought that Whitman's words are like the comforting embrace of a teetering uncle. In his poems, even the most brutal scenes–a murder, a prostitute's beating, a Civil War battle–take on a glow, a shine that somehow assures Liam that everything is justified, all sanctioned by some Supreme Law. "Yes," Walt says to Liam, smiling, "I see your agony, I feel your pain, but none of this matters at all. We're weaned from this earth like the child from the mother's breast. Love it, taste it, embrace it, but never become too attached. All is flux."

Liam smiles with him, happy to have momentarily escaped the troubling thoughts that so constantly tear at his over-examining soul. "If only," Liam thinks as he closes the book and looks across at Mrs. Livingston. "If only I could love everything as completely as Walt does without becoming so damn attached. Attachment. That's my problem. I'm like a fuckin' barnacle."

Then he sighs because he knows that while he possesses an incredible capacity to love, detachment has never been one of his strong suits. Liam's right, like many McGarrity's before him, he holds on to people and possessions like a barnacle to the pylon of a pier. The kid still writes with the pencil he took from my glove compartment, for crying out loud. Some candy-ass shrink might say that's because Mom died when he was young. He'd mumble something about separation anxiety, lack of self-esteem, maybe fear of abandonment. But that ain't true. There were plenty of times *before* Mom died when loss threw Liam for a loop as well. Yeah, shrinks might know a few things, but they've never met a family like the McGarrity's. Shit, a whole team of psych grad students could earn their doctorates studying our ass.

Take Strombastio, for instance, the turtle Liam won for being able to count the highest in Mrs. Frazier's kindergarten class. I'll never forget that damn turtle. Liam came home with him one day, proud as hell. He found an old aquarium in the garage and filled the bottom of it with sand. Then he threw in a couple of rocks and retrieved some lettuce from the fridge for food. For a week, Strombastio and Liam were inseparable. He slept on the bookcase beside our bunk beds, was given free reign in a certain backyard planter, was even fed scraps from the dinner table like some kind of reptilian mutt. At night, Liam would tell the turtle to say its prayers so that it didn't go to the "bad place." For a whole week Liam made me include a turtle named Strombastio in all the bedtime stories I told him. When I asked why we needed to do that, Liam said, "Sean, I know he's not supposed to understand English or anything, but let's just be safe. We don't wanna hurt the little guy's feelings."

But then the next Saturday morning I woke up with Liam beside my bed, holding the lifeless turtle in his hands, asking, "Why? Why? Why?" I guess the little sucker died sometime during the night. My guess is it was overfeeding. Liam gave that thing enough food to feed a pack of turtles. Regardless, the kid was crushed. While Mom and Dad shook off Liam's request for a proper burial for the reptile—replete with coffins, priests, and black-veiled women—Liam was determined to honor his fallen friend. So while I went off to baseball practice, Liam invited the neighborhood kids and conducted the ceremony himself.

First, the viewing. Strombastio at rest in a shoebox, a large leaf of lettuce and a rose by his side. The neighborhood children filed by solemnly, throwing pieces of grass or other backyard shrubbery into the final resting place of the small lifeless shell. Stanley Bradstreet fought back a giggling fit. Then the eulogy. Wearing a black tee-shirt and jeans, Liam got all philosophical about he and Strombastio's brief time together, even going so far as to challenge any of the children present to be as faithful as the fallen reptile. Finally, the burial. In the planter the turtle loved so well, Liam lay him to rest, chanting "Strombastio, Strombastio, Strombastio!" as he piled the soil atop his makeshift sarcophagus.

Mom told me she gave the children ice cream afterwards and

Liam glued two Fudgsicle sticks together in the shape of a cross. He placed it at the head of his fallen comrade and said, "Safe passage, dear friend, safe passage." Every day for a month, the kid put fresh dandelions on the grave, straightening his Fudgsicle-stick cross, making sure the grave was free of rocks and ants and large dirt clods. Then after a particularly vicious night of the Santa Ana winds, Liam awoke to find that the cross on Strombastio's grave had blown away. For an hour he combed the backyard for it, frantically pulling back branches of trees, digging through piles of leaves, muttering under his breath. When his search proved fruitless, he ran to the bathroom, closed the door, and wept. When I knocked and asked him what was the matter, he told me that crosses always confused him then made him sad. When I asked him why, he opened the door a crack and answered.

"Because, Sean, they remind me of crossroads and crossroads are always so confusing. Then I think they look like plus signs, but they don't add anything to your life at all."

So for all his life–from Strombastio to Mom to me–attachment has always caused Liam pain. That's why, a year-and-a-half after I died, Liam tries to push people away with cynicism, solitude, and a lot of Murphy's stout. He knows that if he loves one person he'll have to love them all, and he simply can't stand the thought of losing everyone. Too painful. And as he closes his book and looks around the bus at the other passengers–the mousy businessman, the schizophrenic, the Nicaraguan laborer, the punk-rock girl, and Mrs. Livingston–tears fill Liam's eyes, because he knows no matter how much he loves any of them, no matter how badly he wishes he could help them all, there's nothing he can really do. Then he shakes his head, lowers it to his chest, and prays that he'll find the courage to accept loss and change as completely as Whitman.

But Mrs. Livingston, the old woman in the wheelchair directly across from him, coughs, refolds her lap blanket carefully, and interrupts his prayer.

"So, Isaac," she says to the driver. "How are you this morning?"

"Just fine, Mrs. L, a little tired maybe."

"Yes, yes, I didn't want to jump to any conclusions, but I can see you look a little peeked, young man."

"It's nothing, Mrs. L. How're you doin' this mornin'?"

"Oh, I'm always very well, very well," she responds with a backward wave of her hand, dismissing any talk of herself so she can resume her interrogation of Isaac. "You weren't burnin' the midnight oil last night by any chance, were ya, Isaac? A Christmas party perhaps?"

"No ma'am, nothing like that," he says with a giggle, turning the bus left on to 32nd Avenue. "Just some personal business I had to tend to."

"Well, Liam and I are persons," she says, including Liam with a smile and an open palm. "And we'd be glad to talk you through whatever kept you up last night. It'll help to get it off your chest."

Liam puts his hand up, trying to assure Isaac and Mrs. Livingston he has no desire to be included in their discussion, but they seem to take no notice of him at all. Isaac then looks at both of them in his rearview mirror as if to verify they are indeed people, leans back in his seat, and says in a lowered voice, "You see, Mrs. L, it's my sister…"

Liam closes his Whitman yet again, preparing to hear the worst.

"Yeah, that sister of mine," Isaac adds. "She's not good to her kids, ya know. I told you how she leaves 'em alone at the apartment sometimes, forgets to take 'em to school, stuff like that? Yeah, well, last night my nephew called me about midnight, ya know, 'cuz Angela wasn't home from work yet."

"How old's your nephew, Isaac?" Mrs. Livingston asks. "He's the young one, isn't he?"

"Nah, he's the older one. Eight years old, not a baby or nothin'. He does all right by himself, but he gets worried when it gets late 'cuz he don't feel right about his baby sister sleeping alone. If she wakes up and Angela ain't there, she cries and cries and cries. I only live a few blocks away, ya know, so I went over there and waited for my sister. That's why I'm so tired today. Can't hardly keep my eyes open. Got about two hours sleep is all."

The bus rumbles past a vacant lot dotted with the feces of neighborhood dogs, the local panaderia, and, finally, Rainbow Street South.

"That's not enough sleep for the devil, Isaac, let alone a grown man like you. Terrible. Did your sister finally get home?" she then asks, her arthritic hands folded neatly across her lap. "I mean, the kids are all right now, aren't they?"

"Yes ma'am, yes ma'am, they sure are. Angela didn't get home until after two and she'd been hittin' the T-Bird pretty hard, ya know, so I stayed the night just in case the baby needed anything. Ya know, Mrs. L, I can't understand what she's doing. Those kids are the best…the sweetest kids you'd ever wanna meet. She dudn't know how lucky she is, ya know. I believe I told you, Mrs. Livingston," Isaac says, spotting her in the rear view mirror and speaking even lower, "Hannah and I can't have no children of our own…her insides are all busted up. We'd *kill* to have children and here my sister Angela has two beautiful little ones and she can't think of nothing except that good-for-nothing ex of hers, Billy Blue. And he left her over a *year* ago." He shakes his head as if nothing in this world is to be explained, then says, "Mrs. L, seems like the people that's blessed don't realize it sometimes, and the people that aren't blessed can't think of nothing else."

"That's the truth, young man," the old woman responds with a vigorous nod of her head. "That's most certainly the truth."

Isaac guides the bus to the curb for the next stop and the mousy businessman with the torn coat pocket rises to depart. He mumbles something about welfare mothers as he walks down the aisle and Liam has a strong desire to trip him as he passes, but doesn't. Isaac ignores the man as he departs, then unclasps the belts that hold Mrs. Livingston's chair in place. He wheels her toward the steel platform that will deliver her to the street.

"Here we go, Mrs. L," he says. "Wrap yourself tight with that fine blanket of yours. Cold as hell out today."

He stands behind her as the platform descends to the street with an electric hum, resting his hands on her bowed, decrepit shoulders. She crosses her right hand across her body and pats his hand.

"We all do the best we can, Isaac," she says as the platform descends. "Your sister's just hurting a little bit. That's all. If she doesn't appreciate those children that just means you should appreciate them all the more. That's why the good Lord has seen fit to put you so near to them. And tell that Hannah of yours to keep her head up, there are plenty of children already alive that need loving too. And you never know; the Bible is full of people that thought they couldn't have babies and the Lord blessed them eventually. Sarah, John the Baptist's mom…you just can't tell when or where it might happen. By hook or by crook, that's what my husband used to say. You'll get a child by hook or by crook."

And as the platform screeches to the sidewalk, she squeezes Isaac's hand with finality, like that settles the matter for everyone. Then she turns her chair around and smiles. Isaac smiles in return. Liam watches them through the steamed bus window as they speak in flurries, first one then the other. Isaac's hands flutter like chocolate butterflies as he speaks and Mrs. Livingston points her bony finger like she's shooting her words from it. Then Isaac slaps his knee and waves as the elderly woman wheels away into the cold Colorado morning. Isaac shakes his head as he ascends the steps to his driver's seat, then picks up the microphone and says in his Lou Rawls way, "Next stop, Poinsettia. Ladies and gents, Poinsettia is next."

While the bus traverses the final distance to his stop, Liam pulls the pen from his book and flips through its pages for a suitable passage. Then, as he's done every morning since Rebecca gave him the book, he writes some of Walt's words on his left palm. A note to himself; perhaps a reminder to love without attachment; accept all change if he can. So as the bus whines and lurches, he writes:

I AM THE MATE AND COMPANION OF ALL PEOPLE, ALL JUST AS IMMORTAL AND FATHOMLESS AS MYSELF; THEY DO NOT KNOW HOW IMMORTAL, BUT I KNOW.

Then:

HAS ANY ONE SUPPOSED IT LUCKY TO BE BORN? I HASTEN TO INFORM HIM OR HER IT IS JUST AS LUCKY TO DIE, AND I KNOW IT.

The bus careens to the curb and, feeling comforted by the words and what he's witnessed, Liam stows his pen, puts his book under his arm, and rises.

"See you tomorrow," he says to Isaac, donning his woolen Lakers cap. "Hopefully it'll warm up a bit by then, huh?"

"Tomorrow's Christmas Eve, Liam," Isaac replies. "I ain't workin' tomorrow."

"Yeah, I forgot," Liam says as he brushes past him, putting a hand on his shoulder. "I'm not workin' either. Well, have a Merry Christmas, Isaac. I hope things work out for your sister and Hannah and everybody. Sorry about earlier, just woke up on the wrong side of the bed I guess."

"Hey man, no problem," Isaac responds. "Like Mrs. Livingston says, we're all doin' the best we can. Merry Christmas, Liam. See ya next week."

Before descending the steps to the street, Liam turns around to the rest of the passengers. The schizophrenic still mumbles to himself in the back, the red-caped woman still clenches her unlit pipe in her teeth; the Nicaraguan man still searches the street signs for words that are familiar. For a moment, Liam wishes he could close this bus's doors and talk to all of them, ask them what they want, how they hurt, what can be done to help. He wishes he could drive this bus to a place where things never change, where brothers and mothers and turtles always stay with you, but he knows he simply can't. Instead, he raises his left hand to the passengers, hoping that the words inscribed on his palm or the gesture of inclusion might somehow be of use to all of them. The Nicaraguan man smiles, the red-caped woman nods her head, and the punker with the purple hair smirks and then flips him off.

So Liam departs, shoves his hands in his jacket pockets, and jogs across the street to Big Bob's Market with his book tucked under his arm. He knocks on the glass doors, shuffling from side to side, until Eric Rodriguez, a co-worker, approaches to allow his entrance. Good mornings are exchanged and Liam walks to the storeroom to change into his work uniform. Time to serve some people, time to try and accept all the uncertainty, injustice, and flux in the world. He looks at Whitman's words on his palm then closes his eyes as he tries to commit them to memory.

"Yeah, Seanny," Liam says to me. "They keep bringing me back, digging their claws into me. What the hell's a Mick to do?"

Then–after donning a red apron and putting the Whitman in his locker–Liam strides through the swinging doors to face all the big-oted yet lovable, proud yet vulnerable creatures that exist on the other side of all the doors in the world. Another day in my brother's humble life has begun. It is 6:10 in the morning. The sun has not yet risen.

I also say it is good to fall . . .
battles are lost in the same spirit in which they are won.
                                        –Walt Whitman

Tiny Crosses
by
Liam McGarrity

Aiko, Joe, Kevin, Benny, and I drove to the death site, about an hour and a half away from Deirdre's parents' house, mourning headquarters. Every day we'd assemble at her parents' house trying to think of something to do and every day our impotence mocked us. We needed to act so we piled in the back of Aiko's Toyota long-bed truck and sat against the cold steel bed. It was good to get on the road because after somebody dies people bring glazed hams and mysterious casseroles to your house and there's only so much you can eat, only so much pity you can stomach. I can still see the looks on the faces of the people as they carried their dishes to the door. They would cock their heads sideways–eyes brimming with pathos–and hand me their food in substitution for something they couldn't say, a gesture they were incapable of making.

In the truck as we drove, we joked and laughed and breathed a little easier. No matter the circumstances, it's always nice to get on the road with friends, because there are always other roads, other destinations, and if you wanted to you could keep on driving and nobody could ever stop you. If you mix five men, two cases of beer, a truck, and the open road, anything can be forgotten. At least for a while.

As I drank my beer under the protection of the camper shell, swaying with the turns in the road, it seemed to me that the Pomona freeway was a safe harbor, a refuge from the world outside its lanes. Driving that day, I felt no urge to condemn any god or cosmic justice system gone horribly awry. I felt no desire to fight anyone who slighted me. The Pomona freeway was Switzerland, a pacific place that separated me from all the things that wanted to kill me, all the combatants that demanded my life. I felt safe and wanted to drive forever.

Sean and Aiko (our nickname for Jimmy Sultan) had been friends since high school when Sean transferred to Tryon High after getting kicked out of Thomas Aquinas, the Catholic school. The Aquinas kids called the Tryon High kids "pubes," short for public school and the short hairs. Sean once told me you could fall out of a truck in a public school parking lot and still graduate. He barely made it, though. He was too busy reading to my mother in the hospital and betting on the ponies at the track. He and Aiko would skip class, go visit my mom in the hospital, then head to Santa Anita to try their luck. Sean figured that—no matter how bad things had been in the past— his luck had to change sooner or later. "This is the one," he would tell Aiko. "I can feel it, man. This pony is just like me: pretty, fast, and destined for greatness." He placed every bet just *knowing* that it would be the one that would pay off, and everybody at Tryon High, including Aiko, was pulled to him inexorably because of it. Like Frank Paloma said, Sean was just one of those guys.

As we drove down the Pomona freeway, Aiko put in a bootleg Grateful Dead tape. When the song "I Know You Rider" came on Aiko blasted it loud and we all listened to the words, some of us for the first time. Aiko pounded his hand on the dashboard in time and— as he shook his head and sang along—I realized that he was physically there with the rest of us, but alone in a world none of us knew existed. In the song, Jerry Garcia sang about missing riders when they're gone and how he wished he was a headlight on a northbound train, lighting the way through the cool Colorado rain. Jerry's voice and the music ascended and you could tell that he yearned to become that train, to translate his flesh into something mechanical, cold, unemotional, so that he wouldn't have to miss those riders all the time. It was like his body was a promise he wanted to break, a barrier he wanted to destroy.

We all wanted things to change too, to transform ourselves into something we weren't, to make my brother Sean something he wasn't, to make him come back alive. We dreamed with Jerry and Aiko as they sang, picturing the lonely headlight of a train making its way at midnight along a misty Colorado mountain, and none of us believed for a minute that that train didn't miss the riders too. Aiko turned the music still louder and Jerry sang about how you miss people, how you miss rolling in their arms. And they're gone. Gone, gone.

A couple months after our ride to Temecula I was at Aiko's house for a little shindig where he and his own party band played. As a tribute to Jerry Garcia, their entire repertoire consisted of Grateful Dead tunes. Aiko played guitar and stroked the strings like Bob Weir, hunching his shoulders then pounding downward with closed eyes, his internal vision more acute, colorful, and appealing than anything the physical world could offer. Some of the guests smoked weed, others drank wine, the children played, the music swelled, and aging hippies danced like dervishes before the stage.

With his eyes closed, Aiko sang "I Know You Rider" and only I knew the baggage that song carried, its history and import. The tears were locked under his shut eyes but I knew they were there and that the song was killing him. So–as I stood in a doorway beside the stage–I sang along with him to let him know at least one person heard what he sang. But the song was his alone and he was singing to someone else entirely. Behind his eyes he was thinking about Sean and the rain and all the riders who you miss when they're gone. He sang about futility and impotence and how we all want things to be different. We want to find a better place, but the world will always be as it is now: terrifying but beautiful, deadly, yet filled with enchanting songs. I realize now that Aiko sang about the roots of religion.

Aiko will be singing that song forever, I think. Always chugging through the cool Colorado rain, always yearning for the impossible, his music and art standing alone and timeless, taking him to a place we all yearn to reach. A place where nothing dies.

Joe Quinn sat in the passenger seat beside Aiko, listening to the song and staring straight ahead. The first thing I remember about Joe was an episode at our house when he invited two Mormon missionaries inside to talk some religion. Enrolled at Berkeley at the time, Joe was somewhat of a radical. He wore his blonde hair long, his beard scraggly, and his politics on his sleeve where a peace insignia had been sewn into his jacket. He almost caused a riot at a Rams game one day because he refused to stand for the national anthem when bidden by the announcer to do so. A couple Orange County Nazis (that's what Joe called them anyway) stopped talking on their cell phones to tell him to get up, that his country was being honored. Joe said, "When the people of Columbia and Iraq are allowed to stand, I'll stand too." The prototypical Orange County yuppies (short hair, collared shirts, thick necks) dismissed him with a wave of their hands and went back to their anthems and contraptions, like Americans often do.

When the missionaries came to our house that day, Sean and I sat down, and before those guys could say a word Joe was peppering them with questions.

"How many women occupy seats in the hierarchy of the church?" he asked. "How many wives did Joseph Smith have? What percentage of blacks belong to the church? Is dark skin the curse of Ham? Do you really believe that Utah is the chosen land? Come on, boys, let's hear it…"

Before I knew it those two pimply-faced would-be missionaries were peddling down the street on their ten-speeds as fast as their black polyester-covered legs would carry them. I kind of felt bad for them then, but now I think those Mormons deserved it. No religion should be that clean and straight, that prescribed and sterile. Religions should be messy, Gordian, and packed full of death. Like mine.

As we drove, I realized that what it comes down to is that *none* of us knows what to believe. We're all afraid, looking for a religion.

Me, Kevin, and Benny sat in the back of the truck. Kevin talked about his classes, the little rich brats he taught, and the football team he coached. As he spoke of his days, it occurred to me that he did the exact same thing as his father, a man who died in a plane crash when Kevin was only ten years old. As Kevin spoke, I began to realize that the explanations for men's actions are never quite as simple as we imagine them to be; the reasons they do as they do are often buried with the family that went before them. Sometimes we do things for people that can never appreciate them because they're buried somewhere beneath hundred of pounds of earth, not appreciative at all.

One night Kevin and I were at the Tryon Inn drinking pitchers. As he poured the beer from the fifth pitcher of the night, he told me that he thought his dad's death made him tougher than his peers because he'd survived something none of the others had. I believed that then. After my mom died I too felt stronger than all the untested, but now I see that was just Little Napoleon all puffed up, trying to make himself believe he wasn't afraid of dying. Now I believe that when someone close to you dies it can make you stronger, but it also makes you painfully aware how terribly fragile this pale skin is. Ten feet isn't very far to fall. Ten fuckin' feet. Man, oh, man. Can you believe that shit?

As we exited the freeway onto the Avenida Azura offramp, Benny smiled, put his hand on my shoulder, and handed me another beer. I smiled too, thinking what a rare bird he was. In Orange County, it's not every day you see a bearded, six-foot-three white guy with dreadlocks to the middle of his back. It's hard to believe, but Benny's brother died in a fluke accident too. He dove from a cliff at Lake Mohave, suffered trauma to his chest, and was overcome by the force of the fall, just like Sean.

"Hey man," Benny said to me when I told him Sean had died. "My advice to you is to drink. Heavily. A two or three week beer-buzz is a good way to postpone the pain, dull all those sharp thoughts that keep poking you from the inside. Thoughts lose their bite with enough beers in your system. Don't worry, it's not a cop out. The pain will be there when the beer wears off, but it's better to face it alone, when the relatives and hangers-on are gone. You gotta give it the attention it deserves."

Then he said:

"You see, Liam, it's my experience that living with pain is a lot like living with a beautiful, selfish woman. Cindy Crawford, for instance. You want to go out to dinner or to a party with friends and Cindy, that demanding self-centered bitch, doesn't want to go. And if you're dating someone like Cindy Crawford and she doesn't want to go somewhere, it pretty much means that you ain't going either. It doesn't matter anyway, because if you *do* go out you look like a dwarf next to her. You gotta bring her flowers and candy and sit at her feet in case she needs anything, in case the whim to establish authority strikes her fancy again. I'm tellin' ya, Liam, pain is like Cindy Crawford: you've got to serve it and it alone. You've got your own Cindy Crawford now; you'll see what it's like. For now, drink some beers. Make the bitch wait."

When Aiko's truck approached the construction site where my brother was working, the passengers grew silent. Together, the white bare wood of the newly framed house, the dirt as we left the safe confines of the paved road, and the knowledge that Sean died there, dumbed us. Something happened when we left the pavement that day. It was like we relinquished control of something we'd become accustomed to commanding or directing all our lives. We acquiesced to something beyond our ability to dominate or even begin to understand, like we were bowing blindfolded to some invisible beast that sat waiting behind a curtain that could never be put aside.

In the middle of this valley of custom homes and family wineries, we got out of the truck one by one–timid, shy, terrified of our mortality. We felt insignificant beneath the sky. The fading sun hovered at eye level in the west, the cicadas whirred announcing the close of day, and the grapes said nothing, stoically awaiting their slaughter for wine. They were simply mute sacrifices willing to die for something outside of themselves. An elderly man walked past on the road and waved. He smiled like he knew why we were there and the wave of his hand was a silent endorsement of our journey. As I turned in circles (like Sean had done a few days prior), I absorbed the scene–the rows of grapes, the old man, the incomplete house, the cicadas–trying to take it all inside of me as some futile soul nourishment. As some feeble attempt to feed a part of me that would forever go hungry. It was all I could do.

Only the framing of the house was complete and the intersections of all the two-by-fours formed hundreds of tiny crosses throughout the skeletal monument, like the whole thing was composed of thousands of small altars to which we came to pray. I'm again reminded of something Whitman said, that he discovers as much or more in a framer framing a house as anything. I do too.

It was to be a simple ranch home: three-bedroom, two-bath, a small game room off the back, about fifteen hundred square feet in all. The dirt path that would eventually be the driveway was long and curved, coming back on itself like a snake, taking its time getting from the street to the newly framed house. The nonchalance of the driveway seemed like the tortuous path of salvation to me: filled with detours, backtracks, and snakes, winding slowly, taking us to the uncompleted house where death is.

Sean and his partner, Mike, had completed the framing and Sean had started putting the plywood sheeting on the roof. At the bottom of the roof he was pulling the plywood sheets from his temporary support and cutting them with his saw. After each measurement and cut the sawdust from his labor fell at his feet. I guess the waste at his feet was what killed him, because as he walked to cut another piece of plywood, he slipped on the sawdust and fell over the edge. A crowd gathered and a local rag took a picture of him with the sheet over his head. Some curious gawkers–a few teenagers and a couple housewives–hung around for a bit, then left when all the service vehicles departed. The circus was over. Within forty-eight hours, the owners of the house had hired another company to complete the construction. They were anxious to have it finished before winter.

It seems America will honor a dead man for a day or so, but it always resumes its sure, steady pace afterwards, forgetful of the tragedy it's begotten, like a boxer who kills a man in the ring but fights the next week because he's unable to remember the name of his murdered opponent. We, the laborers, the builders, the sacrificial suckers, we're crushed by the force of America's powerful fists and forgotten. In this country the value of a carpenter's life is almost always lost.

Perhaps the value only remains in the eyes of the men and women who trained the fallen fighter, the survivors who are left to decide what to do with their lives next because they have no contender to mold, nobody to attach themselves to any longer. They've got to fight the world themselves. I know it's probably no use, but with these words I feebly try to stop the monstrous fists of America. If I can't reclaim the value of one laborer's life, if I don't try to grasp the lesson taught by a man who knows he can't beat his opponent but smilingly fights that opponent anyway–there's simply no point to all of this.

Aiko sat alone in his truck with his hands on the steering wheel.

His jerking shoulders evidenced his inability to stop the onslaught that threatened to engulf us all. Silently he wept with his head down, clinging to the wheel. We *all* searched for something to cling to: Kevin grabbed the down tailgate of Aiko's truck, I leaned against a corner of the house, holding the wood with one hand and my Budweiser in the other, Benny picked up rocks and held them tightly, like they were jewels hundreds of people had seen but not yet valued; Joe rubbed the side of his pants like he was trying to remove a stain, and Aiko still held the steering wheel. Without thinking, we did what we could to fight our vulnerability. But nothing seemed to help. We were awash in it.

Then everyone involuntarily came from their spots and began to walk around the house like it was a temple we were unable, perhaps unworthy, to enter. We walked, looked to the incomplete structure, and walked on, slowly circling. Like a true zealot, I was looking for a miracle. I wished with all my soul that our feet would become the blades of a mighty saw that, as we walked in circles, would cut this precious piece of earth away and send it to the sky as an offering, as the seed for a budding religion. I wanted to fly with that piece of earth and my friends and our loss to the heavens, because that unfinished house upon it was a temple, an oracle to which we came looking for some answers, some kind of solace. If my feet would have become saws I could've believed in miracles and the dirt would've been consecrated and people would've flocked to Temecula and that house like pilgrims to Mecca, Knock, and Jerusalem.

But I looked at my feet and saw they were still only feet; I was still only a man. The ground was still part of the earth and I laughed to myself, knowing that I'm no believer.

Although there were no mighty saws on our feet, the rubbing of Joe's hand against the side of his corduroys made a buzzing noise like a small saw at work on wood. His other hand was in his pocket as he kicked stones while circling the house. Occasionally, he looked to the roof where my brother tripped, and shook his head, as if he couldn't believe that a fall from that height could kill a man. As he looked at the incomplete roof, he thought, *Nobody ever thinks about roofs putting you in any danger, that a roof could kill you. Roofs are supposed to protect us from the weather, not create storm systems of their own.*

The clack of a rock hitting the cement foundation made me turn and I saw Benny throwing those valuable rocks of his. "Mother Fucker, miserable piece of fuckin' shit. Whore, bitch, cunt!" he yelled.

The rocks occasionally hit a piece of the framing or the cement, but most of the time they went right through the spaces between all the crosses and came close to hitting a bush, the truck, or one of us as we walked around the site. The others laughed and scurried to get out of his way. I questioned what he was trying to hit, wondered who he was calling names. Then I laughed like the rest because I remembered when we were in the eighth grade and I witnessed the first of Benny's outbursts.

On that occasion, Benny's parents made him believe that our friend Stanley's bike–the Bunn Runner–was stolen, and it was his fault because he left it outside at his house all night. They wanted to teach him a lesson about responsibility so they put the bike in their car and took it to Stanley's house the previous evening. Benny woke the next morning to find the bike gone and was planning how he was going to tell Stanley about the robbery when he saw him ride up on the Bunn Runner. Benny realized that his parents had lied to him and he was pissed. That time–instead of throwing rocks–he threw his backpack at the Dianetics Scientology building at the corner of Irvine and Red Hill. Stanley and I backed up and laughed as Benny hurled a volley of epithets at his parents, L. Ron Hubbard, and the world in general. People honked as they passed, pleased to have something to distract them from their mundane morning commutes.

It was fifteen years later and I thought Benny must have been yelling because he'd been tricked like that time before. Tricked like the rest of us. I'm not sure, though, he could've been screaming at a lot of things. The world provides millions of reasons to curse.

Me, I watched the others and drank my Budweiser as I walked slowly around my circle, still wishing for a miracle or a sign, for the earth to bend one of its rules just once. Every once in awhile I looked at the roof and the ground where Sean must have landed and I wanted to throw some rocks too. Then I looked at the crosses of lumber, the contrast between the dirt and the pavement, my fellow travelers, the driveway, the house on the hill, and the descending sun as it painted a yellow glow around the edges of all the green grape leaves, like it was framing a fragile, priceless picture. The sun bled purple and red across the horizon and looked like a giant heart floating in the sky. It was as if the dying sun was gently blessing us all on its descent and I was chilled by its growing absence.

I huddled my shoulders against the cold and with my Budweiser, my feet that wouldn't change, the songs that wish for the impossible, the fading sun, and the memory of those whose absence makes us yearn for worthy temples, I watched the sun die for the very first time. I'd never before realized how terribly sad the sunset is; it was the most tragic thing I'd ever seen. So—before that mysterious surrender of the heavens that occurs every single day—I shook my head and chuckled to mask my emotion, incredulous that I'd never appreciated the impenetrable miracle of the dusk.

I don't have any idea what to make of this whole scene. It baffles me still. Sometimes it's my personal, poor man's Calvary, a place where the miracle finally showed itself. But most of the time it's just some place that took my brother away last May 16th. I wonder if the people who live in that seemingly ordinary ranch house realize they live on holy ground. Or if that would mean one goddamn thing to them.

FOUR

As you can see, Liam still hasn't gotten over that cross thing. They still confuse him and then make him sad. Amazing how a few years of Sunday Mass and a few dozen CCD classes can fuck somebody up for so long. Leave it to the Catholics to brand you for life. But that legacy doesn't bother the kid; he actually *likes* to puzzle over crosses and stuff. He likes to wonder if there's something eternal in the mundane, something magical in the commonplace. That's his dilemma–he'd rather sit around writing about altars and sacrifice and all that other bullshit, than do anything worthwhile or go anywhere exciting. Meanwhile, most everybody else doesn't give a rat's ass about stuff like that, they're a little more consumed with what's for breakfast, what time the Lakers play, and the other minutiae of everyday life. Take Liam's co-worker, Eric Rodriguez, for instance. He's a perfect example of what I mean.

"I'm talkin' about pussy, man," Eric says as he and Liam walk side by side to the registers, cash boxes in hand. "Snatch, box, the rose petals, the holiest of holies. Know what I'm sayin'? What planet are you from, man? For the love of Pete, get your head out of the clouds, I don't wanna have to explain it *all* to you."

Liam unlocks his register and counts out the money in preparation for his day's work. The Madman (what Eric calls himself) prattles on from the register beside him.

"So there I am, Liam. Al Green on the stereo, a bottle of Andre on the coffee table, and Ivana–that tramp from the club–on the couch next to me, just lookin' for some action. Her eyes were glassy, her lips were willing, and, my brother, the Madman was ready to pounce. I had it all goin' on; know what I mean? Then, out of friggin' nowhere, the bitch's cell phone rings. And I say, 'Let it be, baby, the Madman's the one that's gonna answer the call. Then, if you're lucky, I'm gonna ring your bell too.' Chicks dig that kind of talk, Liam, they lap that shit up. And she says–get this homey–'Just a minute, I'm expecting a call.' "

Eric looks at Liam with arms outspread, an incredulous look on his face. His black hair is slick with gel, combed perfectly backwards. A cloud of Obsession for Men envelops him because, as he says, "I want the bitches to know I'm coming."

"Expecting a call?" he continues. "In the Madman's domain? Excuse me? I don't think so. I didn't spring for Chili's and two bottles of Andre for this bitch to be tellin' me she's expecting a call, know what I mean? So I says, 'All right, bitch, out you go. You expectin' a call? I *expect* you ain't never gonna see *my* sweet ass again. Adios, senorita.' "

Liam chuckles and shakes his head. He's heard so many of these sordid stories he's almost immune.

"Come on, Eric, you never said anything like that."

"Like hell, homey. I kicked that bitch's sorry ass out my door. She'll be back, begging for more before week's end. Trust me. The ladies love it when you show 'em who's in charge. They crave a *real* man. Hey, speakin' of somebody that needs a real man, how 'bout that sweet little thing, Rebecca. Man, I might need a ladder to mount that bitch, but I'm willing to climb. The Madman will…most…def-i-nite-ly…climb. But for some reason or other, she seems immune to the Madman's charms. She walks around here with that tight package, her tits sticking out, and acts like she don't need nobody. I bet she's a lesbo. Carpet muncher. What do you think, Liam?"

"Eric, I think I'm ashamed to be a member of the same species, let alone gender, as you."

"Ah, come on, man, I just say things that other men think. You know you wish you could plow as many fields as I do. Be true to your animal self, Liam. Men just want to chase it, smell it, taste it, then knock it," he says, pounding his fist into an open palm for emphasis. "Simple as that. That's why we're here, man–to plow as many of those sweet-smelling, fertile fields as we can. It's primeval, dude, nothing me or you can do about it."

Thus, Liam's morning passes with the inane banter of Eric Rodriguez and the small talk offered by the housewives and retirees who mostly shop at this hour of the day. Business as usual. Liam jogs to find some baking flour for Mrs. Anderson, suffers through the Madman's off-color joke regarding Jews in Florida, sells dozens of lottery tickets, and occupies himself with the thousand other tasks and responsibilities of a clerk in a neighborhood store. And then, at eleven o'clock, Bob Scallipari–Liam's boss, landlord, and friend–comes bounding through the door.

"My dear, underpaid peasants, how are we this morning?" he says as he sashays toward Eric and Liam with outstretched arms. "The day is glorious, is it not? A bit nippy, true, but crisp in a Chardonnay kind of way. Light, biting, scrumptious."

Bob approaches Eric and engulfs him in a giant bear hug.

"Come, my insecure little heathen, give Big Bob some love."

Eric struggles against his massive employer but is defenseless against Bob's brute strength. "The hair, dude, be careful with the Madman's lid," Eric grumbles. Liam laughs as Bob comes around the counter in front of the register to greet him in kind.

"And you," Bob says to Liam as he embraces him. "How's my little scribe this morning? As one of my misguided, abstemious little friends once said, today is the first day of the rest of your life, Liam. So true. What will you do today? What *will* you do?"

Bob spins Liam around, his left arm wrapped about his shoulder. He points out the window with his right hand and says, "Boys, boys, boys! Breathe deeply, taste the crisp Colorado air, enjoy the spectacle of the day! The snow is on the ground and the pine trees smell lovely. The sun has risen, the air is clear, and I am here. Everything is as it should be. You can almost taste Christmas in the air; the time for the birth is nearly at hand, the birth of the Christ child; the birth of the return of the sun. And who can think of the Christ child and the sun without thinking of the savior on the cross? Hmmm?"

He looks to Eric and then Liam, daring either of them to answer.

"Births and deaths, boys, hope and despair, it's all out there!"

He turns Liam toward him, both hands on his shoulders, and says, "Yes, Liam, even for you. Even for you. Now," he continues as he releases Liam and begins to walk toward the storeroom. "Give me a moment, my dear subjects, and I will spell one of you, give you a chance to go outside and taste the lovely morning. Until then!" he says, raising his arms skyward and spinning down the aisle like a three hundred pound, bearded ballerina. The two clerks look at each other and smile. Big Bob Scallipari has arrived.

Liam was first introduced to Bob five months ago when–while searching for a less expensive place to live–he answered an ad in the *Denver Post* that read:

> For Rent
> N. Den. gst. house
> No ref. nec.
> Love of life req'd
> Call 555-BIGB

Liam and Bob met, a tour of the property was given, and–while sitting around a wicker table in the backyard, sipping a Merlot–a conversation ensued.

"What do you do with your days?" Bob asked, black eyes probing.

"You mean, what do I do for a living?" Liam said.

"If you wish."

"I…ahh…I used to play football for the Broncos, but now I don't do much of anything…except write stories."

"What kind of stories, young man."

"Autobiographical stories, I'd guess you'd call them."

"Published?"

"No, they're kinda just for me."

"Unpublished stories will not pay the rent for my lovely guesthouse, son," Bob said, waving his arm toward the ivy-covered, two-room bungalow.

"No, I guess they won't."

"How do you propose to make money? Or are you independently wealthy? One of those eccentric dot-com billionaires."

"No, I'm not one of those guys. Dot-com don't mean shit to

me, I'm a pencil and paper man. I've got a couple bucks saved up from when I played football, though. Enough for a few months anyway."

"That will not suffice. I am a Bronco fan and I've never heard of you, so you couldn't have made *that* much money. So. You must find a way to pay the bills. Do you propose to make your living as a writer?"

"I haven't thought much about it, to tell you the truth. I'm kinda just feelin' my way right now."

"As a young writer should. Yes. Well, well, well. A writer, a guesthouse, a lack of adequate funds. Yes. Yes. Let's see now. What shall we do about that?"

Bob stood and–hands clasped behind his back, face downward– he began pacing around the table. He walked and mumbled to himself and Liam watched as he clasped and unclasped his hands behind his back. The large man then pulled on his black beard and gesticulated to the heavens, like some invisible oracle rested there. Liam had to stifle a chuckle as this one-man discussion unfolded. For a full minute, the large bearded man paced and questioned, guffawed and grimaced. Then he returned to the table, drained a glass of wine in a gulp, and begin pacing again. He continued.

"Yes. Well. Here's my proposition. Please, I speak quickly, do not interrupt. You will move into the guesthouse. Yes? We will discuss rental terms later. Also, you may work at my place of business, Big Bob's Market. Perhaps you've seen it. Again, we'll discuss terms of your employment at a later date. We will deduct your rent from your wages. Your schedule is your choice. If you write better in the morning, you may work at night. If you write at night, you may work in the morning. Decide which shift works better for you and we'll arrange it. It is nothing to me," he said, waving his arms. Then:

"Now. I do not tolerate absenteeism at the market, nor do I forgive broken promises of any sort. I am straightforward, as you see. If I have a problem with you, your tenancy, or your work ethic, I will discuss the matter directly with you. I expect the same in return. Simple. Let's not complicate matters. Life is difficult enough without our assistance, yes?" he asked, raising his eyebrows. "Now– the house. The toilet runs unless you shake the handle, the pilot on the furnace needs to be relit at least once a fortnight, and a pane in the window off the kitchen needs to be replaced. I will do so this afternoon. Now."

At this, Bob stopped his pacing, poured another glass of wine, and drained it to the dregs. He then turned and stared down at my brother. Liam felt some dramatic pronouncement was about to be made. That's how Bob speaks, in pronouncements.

"Now. The person who occupied this house before you lived here for eighteen years. He was a cantankerous old son of a bitch, but he was my uncle and I loved him. He blasphemed, spat indignities at me, and tried my patience like a plague. But, Liam, he kept his promises. If he said he would prune the roses, it was done. Take the children to the Freedom Park? A certainty. A gruff man, yes, but a man of his word. A man who understood what a promise was. He died three months ago (God rest his soul), and only now am I ready to lease. So, as you might imagine, this place means something to me. You may live here for as long as you like, provided you keep your promises. You see, Liam, I am loyal to a fault. If you betray that loyalty, you will be out. If you do not, we will become friends. I take the enjoyment of life and the pledge of a friend very seriously. *Very* seriously. Both must be honored and savored. So, that is that. Salud! Let's drink to it."

His pronouncements complete, Bob poured two glasses. Liam was caught unawares, puzzled as Bob pulled him to his feet.

"Ahh," Liam stammered. "What…why…how can this work? Why, why are you doing this? I'm not even sure why I answered the ad; I'm not much of a life-lover right now. You might say I've got some issues."

Undeterred, Bob drained his wine and signaled for Liam to do the same. He did so. Bob continued as he poured another glass.

"If you must know, Liam, I have a weakness for writers. The Italians, my countrymen, especially. Dante, Petrarch, Pellegrino, Calvino, I'll even claim Giono as a countryman. Who's to say he isn't? Even as a child I loved writers. I grew up on 43rd Street, a couple blocks over, right next door to the Fantes. Simple family– Italian, Catholic, laborers. Their eldest son, John, was a hero of mine. Local boy done good, you might say. He became a great writer. Under appreciated? Certainly. Mistreated? Of course–all great writers usually are–but he found something noble in the strife of man, something most men fail to see. I loved him for it. If you haven't read his books, let me know, I will loan you mine. They are filled with blood, tears, and joy, like life itself. Yes. Now. I have a weakness for the written word because writing *can* be noble. If you write the base crap that they slap between covers today, I will evict you. Simple. But you seem like a serious man, someone who might write something worthwhile. We'll see. Only time will tell."

Liam felt like a spotlight had been thrust upon him. It was then that Liam knew this man had things to teach him. So, after he'd read all the Fante and Giono in the Scallipari library, Liam asked Bob to read his own stories. He is now Liam's editor. Good thing too, the kid has a tendency to be a little wordy.

"Now," Bob continued, becoming more and more animated with each glass of wine. "On a more banal note–you were the first one to call! Yes, yes, yes! That in itself is proof to me that the fit is right! I believe in destiny! You were destined to come here today. You will write stories in this bungalow and they will be published. It will take time, but that's one thing we have. For now. Because Time is a nasty whore, son, she'll lull you into complacency, make you believe your skin is eternal. Then–BAM–she pulls the rug out from under you like a slapstick comedienne. So, we have time now but we might not have it tomorrow. Such is life. Now. You may move in today if you'd like. You will start work tomorrow. Done."

He rubbed his hands together, then raised them toward Liam, signifying the decisions then made could never be altered. Half in a daze, Liam reached out and shook the outstretched hand of his new benefactor. Then he said, "Oh, by the way, I have a sixty pound Labrador retriever. Will that be a problem?"

"Dammit!" Bob yelled as he snorted and pulled at his beard. He knew that too many grand pronouncements had been made, too many assurances given for him to go back on his word now. Then he looked to the sky, as if consulting that heavenly oracle, and said, "It shan't. I suppose it shan't. Bring the beast if you must."

Liam moved in that afternoon and he and Bob have been friends ever since. This large, gregarious friend now approaches Liam at the registers, insisting Eric now take his break.

"Go now, Mr. Rodriguez," Bob orders. "The young sir and I

have some matters to discuss. Shoo, shoo, off with you now, heathen."

"Thanks, Bob, I could use a smoke. I'll be out front if you need me."

"Fine, fine. But Eric, please, I beg you," Bob says, his hands folded as if in prayer. "Do not harass any potential customers with your catcalls and whistles. I do not want to have to explain to Denver's finest, yet again, your perverted yet harmless habits. Go, go."

Liam stands to bag groceries while Bob takes his position at the register. It is a slow morning. Allison Lobo and her retarded daughter, Joy, enter the store for their daily supply of candy bars and mineral water. An unfamiliar neighborhood child plays Pac-Man near the door while Seymour Goldman, the liquor storeowner, inspects the meats in the deli that the Madman prepared this morning.

"Now. Yes. Ring the bell if you'd like me to open the case for you, Mr. Goldman," Bob yells to the back. "I received some delectable chickens from Greeley yesterday. Beautiful specimens."

Liam stands at the end of the conveyor belt and reads an article in a tabloid concerning the possible possession of Bill Gates by Beelzebub. Liam nods. He and I have always had our suspicions.

"Now, Liam," Bob says. "As for you. Yes. Well. How was your evening? Productive? Did you string a succession of beautiful words together? Dazzle the minds of readers not yet born? Hmmm?" Then, hoping to stop a lie before it is uttered, he continues. "I know you didn't, Liam, your lights were out at nine and I spoke with Dick Hackett at the coffee shop this morning. Our little friend told me you were at the pub all evening. And don't feed me any nonsense about editing stories there or reading your *Leaves* there. Reading and writing in a bar? Self-delusion, Liam, self-delusion. The only worthwhile writing in a bar is on the menu, Liam, and at Rainbow Street South they can't even offer that. Yes. I'm worried about you. You've completed the cycle of stories. I edited the last of them weeks ago. What will you do with them now? Huh? What will you do?"

Liam returns the tabloid to the rack and shrugs his shoulders. "I don't know, Bob, what the hell am I supposed to do?"

"You're supposed to let other people read them, son; an agent, a publisher, an editor of a magazine. A writer needs an audience of more than one, Liam. I know, I know, you feel exposed in them, naked, vulnerable. Well. Get used to it. The best writing exposes, lays the soul bare on the page. I know that Little Napoleon of yours wants to be published. Don't lie to me, I've seen him. He may have died that day in May, but he's reborn periodically, isn't he?"

Liam looks at him in silence.

"Yes, I thought so. I know Little Napoleon wants exposure, someone to tell him the stories are beautiful, poignant, and lyrical. Yes, Liam, I know Little Napoleon wants the stories published because then he can live forever, and that's all anybody's ego wants. Well. We shan't argue the point now. This week is for births, holidays, the exchange of gifts, and my party tonight. I expect you there at seven-thirty sharp. I will need help with the wine and the bread and Linda expects you to sample the hors d'oeuvres before the other guests arrive."

"By the by," Bob continues. "You know I admire the expedient tactics of intrigue employed by my countryman, Machiavelli, and, knowing this, it should come as no surprise to you that I have utilized everything in my power to get what my wife, Linda, and I desire. And since you refuse to shake yourself from this dormancy of the soul, we have taken steps to do it for you. Yes. Well. Last week, I took the liberty of making copies of all your stories. I sent one copy to a small publisher in New York. Linda suggested I give another copy to Rebecca Kelly for her perusal. As you might know, Rebecca has been curious why her amply baited hook has not landed you and Linda was right, the stories were the best way to explain. It's done. No reason to complain now."

Incredulous, Liam begins to protest, but is stopped by Bob's outstretched hand. His pronouncements continue.

"Now. Rebecca told me yesterday that she was almost done reading them so she should be ready to discuss them over a fine Cabernet tonight at the party. Yes, she will be there also. Don't look so shocked, young man. After all, she is an employee of mine as well. Yes. Well. Tonight, we will ruminate over your prose as we partake of the wine of our cellar, the bread of our oven, the pleasure of our garden. I will not hear any excuses. If you wish me to remain a friend, you will not excuse yourself from the party. If you do not come, I will consider our friendship and business relationship over. Even the loveliest bird must be pushed from the nest if it's ever to fly. It is time."

Lost, Liam looks to the ceiling (searching for me) then to his hands to see if Whitman can help him accept the fact that the woman he simultaneously desires and fears has seen into the darkest parts of his soul, partaken of his innermost secrets. And as if that's not enough, the Whitman epigrams at the beginning of each story are sure to show her just how much the book she gave him has become in his life. Confused and cornered, he looks at the poetry on his palm to get his bearings, but a day of bagging groceries and handling money has erased most of what was there just hours before. The only words he can make out are, "mate," "companion," and "lucky."

You're on your own, bro.

"Thanks, Sean, thanks, Walt," Liam mumbles. "Where the hell are you when I really need you?"

Then, as if on cue, Rebecca Kelly walks through the door that the Madman has held open for her. As she passes, Eric tries to smell her hair, then he watches her ass as she enters the store. He gives Liam the A-OK sign, mouths the word, "Perfect," and follows her in. With her auburn hair flowing from beneath her black wool cap, she strides confidently toward Bob and Liam. Beneath her arm Liam sees a stack of papers, the first of which reads, "The Death of Little Napoleon." He feels nauseous.

Grinning, she says, "Good morning, boys, how are we today?"

She walks past Liam and kisses Bob on the cheek. They share a conspiratorial smile as she makes her way to the storeroom.

"We're just fine," Bob responds. "Just fine, little flower. In fact, we were speaking of literature and wine and bread and love. Weren't we, Liam?"

Liam stares at him, red with embarrassment.

"Yes. Well," Bob continues. "At least one of us was."

As Liam turns to watch Rebecca walk away, he feels like every wall he's built, every fortification he's erected in the past eighteen months, has been destroyed in a single moment. Besides the sun and the wind and my death, Liam now knows that Rebecca

Kelly and Bob Scallipari are two more forces of nature against which he is powerless.

"This world," he mumbles to me, reaching skyward like he's trying to grab my hand. "It's killin' me, Seanny. It's fuckin' killin' me."

"Yes. Well," Bob says with a laugh. "Such is life."

"Tell me about it," Eric offers.

And Rebecca walks down the aisle with Liam's stories clutched to her bosom, smiling at the disturbance her arrival has caused. Liam follows her with his eyes, the lightness in his stomach almost unbearable. He breathes deeply, trying to ease his discomfort, but understands he has no chance at all. Once again, my brother Liam is defenseless.

My right hand points to landscapes of continents,
and a plain public road.
Not I, not anyone else can travel that road for you.
You must travel it for yourself.

—Walt Whitman

Plain Roads and the Rebels Who Tread upon Them
by
Liam McGarrity

I used to shadowbox a life-size poster of Muhammad Ali every night before I went to sleep. It was pinned to the wall at the foot of the bunk beds Sean and I shared. "Ali," Sean said as he unrolled the poster. "The greatest athlete the world has ever known." On the poster, the Champ wore oversized white trunks with cherry red gloves. The sweat poured down his face and torso while the muscles in his biceps and thighs glistened and shone. I thought he looked like a leopard one instant, a shark the next. He was liquid yet solid, hard yet graceful as a dove. His eyes spoke of passion, anger, and amazement, like if he didn't whoop your ass with his fists, he could outrun, outthink, or out laugh you just as well. The first time Sean unrolled that poster it scared the hell out of me, but over time I'd grown used to it and as long as he stayed flat on the wall, Ali didn't scare me anymore. In fact, after I studied the poster and Sean told me some stories about him, I started to like the Champ.

As I lay in bed after the sparring match I could see his eyes through the wooden slats at the foot of my bed, the sweat forever rolling down that forever focused face. He stared at me from between the slats like he was in a darkened jail cell, still fighting. I couldn't help but wonder what it must have been like for the Champ to go to jail instead of Vietnam, the reasons he refused to follow the others. Sean told me he went to jail because he was a Muslim and saw no reason for killing someone who'd done him no harm. As a young boy lying on that bed, I had no idea who or what a Muslim was, but whatever they were, I thought they made a lot of sense.

After my sparring match, I put my red Everlast boxing gloves (a birthday present from Sean) just inside the bedroom door because I knew Sean would trip over them and say something he wasn't supposed to say. Around midnight, the bedroom door opened and I saw the light at the foot of the door suddenly change from a thin line to a wedge. Sean and his shadow then broke the light wedge, tripping on the gloves, stumbling into the darkness of the room.

"Goddammit, Liam," Sean yelled. "I told you not to leave the friggin' gloves in the doorway."

Sean threw the gloves on my bed and Curley, my off-white mongrel, stood up, moved to the other side of my feet, and laid back down. Sean undressed slowly in the dark, finally climbing into the bed below mine. A long time before I'd promised not to tell Mom and Dad that he wore no clothes at night. Sean was always breaking the rules. He slept in the nude, snuck out the bedroom window at night, and skipped school to bet the ponies at Los Al.

"Hey Sean, you sleeping?" I whispered.

"Yeah Liam, I'm just talking in my sleep," he replied.

"Me and you goin' to church tomorrow?" I asked.

"Yeah."

"Why do we go to church, Sean?"

"Because I promised Mom. And we're Catholic."

"What does that mean?"

"It means we go to Mass on Sundays."

"Ain't we Irish?"

"Yeah, we're Irish too."

"So really we're only half Catholic. Right?"

"No, Liam. We're all Irish and all Catholic. Irish Catholic, that's us. A couple of California Micks."

"Well, at school Ms. Small told us that two halves make one," I answered. "If we're all Catholic, we can't be anything else. If we're all Irish, we can't be anything else either. If we're all Irish *and* all Catholic we'd be two people total. I think we're only half each because two only goes into one half a time."

By this time I was leaning over the edge of the bed, peering down on my brother to see if he understood what I was saying. He had his eyes closed and was trying to fight back a smile. I could see the tan line on his stomach in the semi-dark.

"Liam, Irish is a nationality. Catholicism is a religion. We can be both Irish and Catholic then. You see?"

"So . . . so we couldn't be all Irish and all German then, right?"

"Exactly."

"Well, my friend Steve told me that he's English, Scottish, German, and Spanish. What does that make him?"

"That makes him a mutt."

"Like Curley?" I said, and Curley pricked up his ears and craned his head sideways like he was trying to understand our whispered words.

"Just like Curley," Sean responded.

I told Sean I couldn't wait to call Steve a dog Monday at school, to inform him about the canine lineage in his family's past. Sean was lying on his back with his eyes closed.

"You do that, bro," he said as he pursed his lips with laughter. "Go to sleep, Liam. It's late."

* * *

The next morning Sean and I were off to church. We dressed casually in corduroy shorts, T-shirts, and open-toed sandals. When I asked Sean if we'd get in trouble for not dressing up for church, he said, "Champ, Jesus never wore a tie, a collared shirt, or a blazer. He never heard of Polo or cared about physical appearances, so neither will we. Fuck it."

The other parishioners felt much differently than Sean about proper church attire. The men wore unyielding polyester suits, gold crosses on their lapels, white hankies in their pockets. The women wore flowered dresses with white high heels and olive nylons pulled way past their knees. They nudged their partners and snickered at their neighbors, silently judging them where they sat. The kids poked each other in the ribs and played with toy cars and Barbies, choking on their clip-on ties and high-necked dresses. Sean and I sauntered by in our shorts, heads high, defiant. We stuck out like sore thumbs. When we passed Mrs. Carlyle, she shook her head and sighed, pushing her gray hair up with a nervous hand. It was like she thought God would punish the entire congregation for Sean's impious dress.

Sean said, "Good morning, Mrs. Carlyle."

She put her fingers to her lips as if his voice would further enrage the Almighty. Sean loved it because he wanted to show everyone that he (and I, because I was his younger brother and did everything he did) was different than them, that he played by rules that only he and the Lord Almighty understood and that all the properly suited and shod were mindless followers, just money lenders in the temple. Sean loved symbolic gestures.

St. Cecilia's Church was a long, rectangular, lugubrious affair that had the architectural creativity of a penitentiary or a reform school, maybe a hard-edged coffin. It was three stories high with stained-glass windows that were so tiny you couldn't tell what was being portrayed in them. I squinted at them from the car but all I saw was a kaleidoscope of bright colors, the outlines of a few bodies, and the cross. The message was obscured. Why was the stained glass so distant and nondescript? I wondered. Why weren't the windows larger, more celebratory? Why aren't the stories contained in them readable to the poor saps below? I wanted the stained-glass windows to be closer to me and more immediate, more poignant, like a good story.

The inside of the church was just as depressing, if not more so than the exterior. Every time I entered church and saw the ponderous wood doors with their heavy deadbolts, I was mystified. Why did they have to lock the doors to the church? I thought they *wanted* people to come there. That's what the priests said every Sunday anyway. The pews were hard stained wood with high backs so that I had to sit up to see over the edge of them. They had no cushions on them so it only took about fifteen minutes for my butt to go numb. The seats were right out of some medieval monastery, there to make the congregation suffer, like the Church thought it would make our asses pay for our sins. That'll show those sinners.

The only things that enlivened the monotonous brick walls were the distant stained-glass windows I'd seen from the car. It pissed me off that I still couldn't make out the scenes in them. Stained-glass windows used to tell stories to the illiterate masses because they were unable to read the Bible. But I would've had to be a giant, some kind of monster to be tall enough to read the stories in St. Cecilia's stained-glass windows. I wanted the glass to dominate the sterile atmosphere inside, to stretch from floor to rooftop so that the sun had a chance to do its thing, so that it could make the stories in the glass come alive to all the people below. Because the white sunlight is supposed to be the holy spirit and the light of the spirit should filter through the pictures in the glass and the resulting colors as they splash over you, as they bathe the congregation in the Trinity itself, are supposed to be like waves of stories washing over you eternally. At least that's what Sean told me.

But the light from the St. Cecilia windows was small and impotent, futilely dying on the red brick on the other side of the church, about twenty feet overhead. The light was useless up there and it left the masses empty, story-less, questioning beneath the light like dogs whose owners had abandoned them although they'd committed no transgression they could recall.

We went to the nine-thirty Mass. The Mass before ours was delivered in Vietnamese because there's a large Vietnamese population in Tryon. The priest who delivered the previous Mass and ours was named Father Francois Nguyen, a Vietnamese immigrant. I always wondered if he was the father of Peter Nguyen, a kid that played on my basketball team at school. But Sean told me later he couldn't be his dad because priests can't have any children. That made no sense to me because everybody called them Father. At our basketball games, before we went out for the opening tip-off, our coach would say, "Let's root for Pete," and on three we would all yell "WIN!" I wondered if the altar boys would chant the same thing before Father Francois came out to say Mass. You know, win one for Christ, something like that.

Because of his accent, you couldn't understand a thing Father Nguyen said. Sean and I stood in the back of the church where the speakers screeched with feedback and his words ricocheted off the high ceiling and brick facade. In the back of St. Cecilia's you couldn't understand a priest who spoke clear English, let alone Father Nguyen, who called Mary, "Da Bwesset Wawin." Sean told me that no matter what language the priest is speaking, the second-best place to be in a Catholic church is right by the back door. The best place, he said, was *out* the back door.

Since I couldn't understand a word the priest was saying, I watched all the people around me, hoping their expressions might give me a clue as to what was happening up front. But they were mostly expressionless, no help at all. Then I studied the church itself. On our side there was a statue of St. Cecilia, an altar where you could light candles for the dead, and a couple confessionals. Above them, I saw the stages of the cross carved in wood. They encircled the church, displaying the near-naked Jesus stumbling up the road to his death on Calvary. Nobody else seemed to notice the brutality of the carvings. Blood streaming down his face, the soldiers sneering at him, the scrapes and cuts on his knees evidence of his numerous falls. Nobody knew that I had nightmares where I tried to help him up the hill but couldn't get past the spitting crowds and Roman soldiers who, like the congregation today, looked at their watches a lot. In the nightmare I duck the spit and scream at those damn ancient peasants that it isn't time, it isn't time, and I cry because wristwatches aren't supposed to be invented yet, this emaciated man shouldn't be killed yet. But the people just spit and laugh and look at their watches some more, and it doesn't seem to bother Jesus at all. He winks at me in the dream, like he knew it would happen that way all the time.

There was a giant crucifix behind the altar whose base looked like it was planted in Father Nguyen's head below it. Jesus wore this pathetic grin and had his head pitched sideways, like he was looking for some help, somebody to bail him out of this mess he'd found himself in. His rib cage protruded against his skin and his loincloth barely covered anything. The blood rolled down his face from the crown of thorns. His hair was oiled and combed and I thought what a lie that was, like the Romans would doll him up before they killed him. Of course he was barefoot and his feet had nails going through them. Once, when I asked Sean about the crucifix, all he said was, "Liam, some people have some serious balls. That's what I think about when I think about Jesus. A man with balls enough to listen to nobody else, a man who let the voice inside of him dictate his every move."

Below Jesus was this Vietnamese priest. In the decade or so

since he'd left Vietnam, Father Francois had become the most American of Americans. In his homilies, he wondered what effect the Vietnam War had on the American psyche, debated the fairness of certain immigration policies, campaigned on behalf of several Orange County conservatives. Out of church, his favorite pastime was arguing the relative merits of American films dealing with Vietnam. Sean and I liked *The Deer Hunter* but thought *Apocalypse Now* was the best because we both read *Heart of Darkness* first and appreciated a little craziness in our movies and fiction. Father Francois had a fondness for *The Green Berets* because John Wayne, a fellow Orange County resident, was the star.

Father Francois stood at the base of the crucifix, his hands folded across his paunch, his closed eyes supposed to signify some kind of piety as he spoke. The contrast between the priest and Jesus confused me. One man with a cross planted in his head, protected behind these high brick walls and high black collar, professing to speak for that man on the cross behind him. The other man unprotected, out in the sun, at the will of the elements and unafraid, stumbling up that hill and forgiving the people who spat upon him on the way. I saw all this and realized that Father Nguyen and Jesus had little in common and if they met each other on the streets that day the priest probably wouldn't even nod his head in acknowledgment. But then again I couldn't imagine them ever traveling the same road in the first place.

Then my eyes fell on Sean. Unlike me, he never looked at the priest. His head swept the congregation looking for chicks. He was looking at Chantal Robbins and her black hair and thick eyelashes, then Michelle Jenkins and her kinky blonde hair and the white peach fuzz that lined her upper thighs. He always smiled at the women and they sensed it and turned around, smiling in return. They couldn't resist him.

Sean later told me that Catholic girls are all one way or all the other and that like Billy Joel said; sometimes they start way too late. It was about ten years before I realized what he meant. I was in Jacqueline Joyce's bed at the time. Her grandfather was from Ireland and she was the chairperson of the Catholic Club at a local community college. When I met her at a party, I told her my dad was from Cork and she almost attacked me right there. In her bedroom, there was a silver crucifix above her door to ward off all those demons that have a tendency to go after Catholics at night. But in her nightstand there was a pack of condoms and a vibrator. To ward off other demons, I guess. When I saw that vibrator I thought of what Sean said ten years before, then laughed with my legs kicked up toward my chest. In response to Jacqueline's query as to what I found so funny, I simply shook my head and said, "Nothing."

By the way, Billy Joel was right about another thing: only the good die young. Only the good die young. *ONLY THE GOOD DIE YOUNG!*

Jesus, it feels good to scream at the sun every once in awhile.

* * *

Sean and I only stayed about twenty minutes when he gave me the "let's go" pull of the head. It was like I was on a string attached to that pug nose of his; when he turned I was pulled into his wake. I followed him like a terrier, hoping one of my friends would see me walking out of Mass early with my older brother, like we were James Dean and Muhammad Ali, just a couple more guys too cool to care.

We drove to see Tom Boyle at the dairy where he worked because Sean didn't like to stay for communion. ("Too weird," he said.) Sean and Tom Boyle both went to Thomas Aquinas High School until their junior years when Sean was kicked out for insubordination, indolence, and what the priest in charge of discipline said was, "a generally mutinous attitude toward authority as a whole." Sean and Tom stayed friends afterwards and talked a lot about the differences between public and private schools. Tom thought that the biggest difference was that Sean could see girls wearing miniskirts, whereas at Aquinas they wore the long plaid skirts that had been part of the uniform since the school's inception in the fifties. Tom dreamed of seeing all the legs of the nubile women in public school. His imagination got the best of him and, in his mind, not only were the students beautiful and scantily clad, but even the teachers and secretaries showcased tan, muscular bodies there to tempt his young lusts. Tom would look at his starched white shirt and blue tie and curse he was born Catholic at all.

When we arrived at Grievey's Dairy, Sean gave me a Coke and some chocolate ice cream that came in a small cardboard container that said it served four. I usually polished it off in one sitting. Sean and Tom usually cracked open some Budweisers and acted like world-weary men, like their age was an ailment that could be easily rectified with the consumption of alcohol. They steeled their eyes and sipped the beers silently, like they were contemplating things that could only be understood by beer drinkers. Tom told us that over the course of one Saturday—from dawn when he opened until 8:00 P.M. when he closed—he drank twenty-eight Budweisers. That was his record.

"That's right, boys. Twenty-eight beers in one day," he said.

At the end of the night he stacked the beers in a pyramid, eight on the bottom row, then seven, six, etc. Right before closing time he looked at the pyramid and—being reminded of pins in a bowling alley—he rolled through the cans like a drunken human bowling ball and passed out beneath the pile, exhausted from the effort. When he woke up, Mr. La Scala (the owner of Grievey's) was standing over him and Tom said it looked like he was an angel because the fluorescent lights shone from the back of his head like a halo. Tom said he smiled because he felt light and happy and his proof for the existence of angels was finally unequivocal. He was so comfortable looking at that angelic figure that he thought he must be dead, killed by the euphoria of over a case of beer combined with the disorientation of a few spins on the ground.

But the illusion of angels and heaven lasted only until Mr. La Scala slapped him twice across the face—once with each hand—then threw him over his shoulder and carried him to his car. Mr. La Scala took Tom home where he had to explain to his mother why her underage son was drunk on a Saturday, passed out on his bed, mumbling something about picking up a two-ten split.

Tom didn't steal as many beers as he used to, but he and Sean still tipped a few every Sunday. I wondered how Mr. La Scala ever made a dime at a dairy where his sole employee was also his biggest problem, drinking and eating everything within his grasp. My dad would say that Tom Boyle working at that dairy was like the fox guarding the henhouse, but at the time I didn't care what Tom and Sean drank or how much was pilfered from a company till. I was hanging out with my brother and his buddy while all my friends were either at church or playing kids' games somewhere, and nothing could be better than that.

As they sipped their beers Tom and Sean talked about Chantal, Michelle, and the other girls at church. Then they debated whether or not they would meet at Tryon Meadows Park that evening. Sean said he couldn't because he had to go visit Mom in the hospital. Tom asked how she was; he hadn't visited in a couple of weeks. Sean looked at me sideways and said, "All right, I guess."

Though I knew he was lying, I swung my feet from the counter and ate my ice cream, pretending I didn't hear. I wanted to get the hell away from that conversation, anywhere to avoid the unappetizing possibilities the rest of that talk offered, but there was only the ice cream and the Coke and the Budweisers and the outdated dairy and the hospital. I wished I could fall into that ice cream carton, that it was large enough for me to lose myself there. The soft rolling canyons, the sweetness and predictability in the carton of Carnation ice cream appealed to me, as if it presented possibilities of childish indulgence the world itself did not.

Then I began to realize that chocolate ice cream, Cokes, Budweisers, any kind of food or drink you enjoy, anything you shove down your throat in a vain attempt to fill something unfillable, *can* help you forget things, but only for the length of time it takes to devour it. Because you don't really forget, you're just fooling yourself, trying to make yourself believe that your life is intact, and when you're done with the meal your life remains exactly as it was before. There's never enough ice cream or beer to make you completely forget. You bite and eat, you sip and drink and the chocolate runs down your chin and the beer spills out your lips and it's all sticky on your face and you're full but not really and there's another quart of ice cream, another six-pack of beer, and nothing really helps. No matter how much you eat or drink, the holes are always there.

After we'd finished our food Sean told me to thank Tom and I did and we got in the car and honked at him as we left. I asked Sean if we were going home and he smiled because he knew that I knew we weren't. We drove across town, past the orange groves that bordered Tryon's south side, up Palm-lined Carver Lane, into Tryon Hills, where the rich people lived.

Unlike the roads in our neighborhood, the roads in Tryon Hills were curvy and narrow, like the designer of them wasn't sure where he wanted to go until he laid the pavement where his feet then stood. Although I'd ridden through those hills countless times, when we emerged from each turn the approaching piece of road surprised me, like it was a stretch newly invented for Sean and me. The ever-changing road and the speed at which we drove scared me a bit, but did not faze Sean in the least. He accelerated his Mustang halfway through each curve, eager to see what kind of road stretched beyond his line of sight.

We drove to Half Mile Hill which is just what its name implies: a hill that descends down for half a mile until it dead-ends into a gate that has a big NO TRESPASSING sign emblazoned upon it. The unpaved road behind the gate was used by the Levine Company to survey the thousands of acres of orange trees they used to cultivate. But oranges weren't as profitable as tract homes, so the Levine Company gave up farming and started building houses instead. Starting just south of Tryon, they began cutting down the orange trees so they could build a suburb town called Levine. In Levine you can go down any street and think you're on your own street, that the next house is yours, because they all look the same: three to four bedrooms, prominent garage doors, white or tan or some other neutral color, some other sign of blandness. Simply by living there, Levine's residents tacitly endorse the belief that safety is better than passion, that uniformity beats individuality.

The grove of trees at the bottom of Half Mile Hill was one of the last in all of southern Orange County that the Levine Company hadn't destroyed yet. When Sean and I got to the bottom of the hill we parked in the dirt on the side and hopped over the gate right above the sign that told us to stay out. Sean told me not to let a piece of steel tell me what I should or should not do. The dirt road went out before us like a long lazy trapezoid whose end, though chased interminably, would continue to recede into the distance. We were the only ones on it. Towering eucalyptus trees bordered the lane on either side and when you broke open their leaves and held them to your nose they smelled like squeezed lemons. Behind the eucalyptus were the rows and rows of orange trees and when I asked Sean if we would get in trouble if we got caught out there, he told me that, first of all, they could never catch us. Second, we had to be there to see the orange groves before they razed them all to build more condominiums or golf courses, before lakes with cement bottoms and filters replace the pond over the ridge. Before this abandoned, unpaved road becomes just another anonymous Levine street with anonymous people upon it.

I looked around at the orange and eucalyptus trees, at the dirt beneath my feet, like I would be the last one to see any of it, like if I was called upon I could be the final witness to this vanishing world. The trees were majestic and stoic in the denial of what was going to happen to them. They were still, with no wind to give them a voice. Nameless birds sang above us in the trees. I couldn't see the birds, so each distinct call was like the ethereal echo of a fleeting voice trying to be heard and remembered, never realizing that the call lives on long after the throat that gave it utterance. Never knowing that each singer has to learn that lesson anew.

The cicadas whirred and I now think of what Basho said, that though the voice of the cicada will die soon, it shows no sign of it. Some people sing loud and strong right to the end, just like a cicada. The echoes of a loud life ring forever, while the timid voice of a coward is lost long before the end of his time.

I told Sean that I couldn't hear any cars and he said, "Exactly." We walked and Sean told me that Mom was really sick and I said I knew. He told me that she might not live and I looked at my shoes and the dirt that was raised from my steps and said nothing. He told me that things would be all right and I didn't believe him. He reached out his hand for mine and I was eleven years old, much too old for that, but I held his hand anyway and looked straight ahead because I didn't want him to see my tears and not a word was spoken. His hands were not yet calloused from the workaday world; he'd not yet graduated from high school. I cried as quietly as possible, trying to imagine an unimaginable tomorrow. Sean held my hand firmly but tenderly, not drawing attention to my weakness. We walked and I cried and, no matter what words I use, I can't even begin to tell you how much I loved him.

Silently, we walked farther along that path, farther into the groves, and I wasn't just sad about my mom. I was sad that the trees would be slaughtered, sad that the Champ had to go to jail, sad that I was both Irish and Catholic because on some level I realized all that meant. I was sad that Tom was always at that damn dairy, that the priest spoke words I cannot understand, sad that we were killing all the rebels still; and, finally, I was sad that the straight roads are always paved and crowded and I can't control my fear of the winding, unpredictable paths. And it was the first time that the sadness of the world came over me and I couldn't stop crying because all the weight was there.

After a few minutes the tears began to dry in rivulets on my face. I licked the salty moisture from my upper lip. When I looked at Sean and saw that we were still holding hands, I was surprised. I let go because I was ashamed and Sean smiled at me so that I knew it was okay, that it was just me and him on this quiet path. He rubbed my black hair affectionately. I began to run back to the car because we always raced on Sundays and I needed a head start.

"Race ya to the car," I yelled, already five yards ahead of him.

I ran and knew that he could catch me at any time though he never would. I heard his footsteps behind me and strained to run faster. He told me he was going to catch me and I looked over my shoulder and ran faster still, realizing that you can always run faster than you think, always do more than what you thought possible, even when the sadness is upon you. You've just got to have a rebel to convince you it's true, someone to take you to a place beyond the fences and their warnings, beyond the tract homes, beyond the safe superhighways that go straight forever. A rebel like Sean can convince you to move beyond the confines of this paltry flesh, to a place whose existence you never even hoped could exist. A place at the end of an abandoned road.

I touched the gate with the NO TRESPASSING sign on it and put my arms up in victory and sang, "I am the champion." Sean said that I *was* a champion and I put my arms up like Muhammad Ali and I swooned and punched the air like I was the Champ, the greatest of all time, like I too would never be cowed by whatever is piled upon me.

Even though all the weight was still there. Even though I knew Sean let me win.

The Party

FIVE

I told you before that what's lost to the flesh is multiplied in the spirit a million fold. And it is. But for guys like me, the ones that die while still enjoying the flesh quite a bit, the transition can be a little rough. Again, I don't want to go Swayze on you, but that's part of the reason I'm still here: I just needed a little time to break free, a little time to shake loose from the demands of the flesh.

But I'm no different from anybody in the McGarrity clan. We were always a fleshy crowd, a little enamored with the body and the appetites. Personally, what I miss most are the ordinary things. Like a ham and mustard sandwich on sourdough or a cold Coors after a long day's work in the sun. Or the light touch of Deirdre's hand on my freshly-shaven face, a lusty smile between us speaking of passionate hours we'd already shared. Yeah, or the smell of Erin and Brigid's wet hair when they've just come from the tub. One on either side of me, I would read *Goodnight Moon* or *Curious George* to them, feeling their cotton pajamas rubbing against my bare chest. The crickets outside the trailer serenaded us as both of the girls laughed at George's antics or bid the moon goodnight. Their hands rested on my stomach as they sniffled or laughed and then inhaled deeply in that first moment of sleep. I could watch and listen to those kids sleep for hours on end. Christ, those things still kill me.

But I started on this whole flesh business because–as I watch Liam peeking in the Scallipari's kitchen window–I can't help but think of food. And though I was a skinny man, I was a McGarrity, and the McGarrity's are legendary eaters. As a neighbor of my grandfather in Ballincollig used to say, "The only things that'll ever wear out on the McGarrity's are their teeth and their arseholes."

Liam knocks on the door, glares through the window, and–though he's kind of lost his appetite since I died–his mouth is suddenly watering. Linda, Bob's diminutive wife, opens the door and wipes the hair from her eyes with the palm of her flour-caked hand.

"Come in, Liam, come in," she says. "Join the chaos."

Liam kisses her cheek and smells flour on her skin and wine on her breath. The pumpkin and nutmeg soup simmers in a large tureen on the stove and Liam inhales its robust thickness from afar, almost tasting the copper heartiness of it as it tries to combat the bite of the air outside. The warmth in the kitchen is intense and Liam watches as Linda, Bob, Guillermo (a cousin from Fort Collins), and Bob's father scuttle in and out of the kitchen, turning sideways to avoid one another in the doorway as they pass–joking, slapping, and touching as they go. The room is aflutter with the frantic activity that precedes all joyous occasions.

Bob's seven-year-old daughter, Rosemary, scampers in and out with her cousins, chastised by a parent, bidden by some distant relation to perform some impossible task. The children giggle and run and ignore the adults. Good for them. Bob blows dust from the labels of the dozen bottles of wine–from gilded bronze to deep plum in color–that line the counter next to the sink. He examines the handwritten labels from the wine he's produced with his own toil, unconsciously licking his lips and smiling with the perusal of each. Two large baking sheets filled with walnut, chocolate, and gingerbread cookies (frosted designs emblazoned across them) sit upon the counter beside the soup until Vincent (Bob's fourteen-year-old son) lifts them above his head and takes them into the dining room with the others. Linda opens the old O'Keefe and Merritt oven and waves of heat billow from its depths, carrying the smell of golden homemade bread through the kitchen until Liam must close his eyes to inhale. The windows in the kitchen are steamed and Liam opens his eyes and watches the ice on the outside windowsill melt across the panes. The house itself seems alive, like the frenetic actions of the people in its depths have infused the plaster, brick, and wood with a life unto itself. From just inside the back door, Liam watches with wonder. He is reminded of other kitchens in other times.

"Come, Liam," Linda beckons. "The appetizers are on the table already and we want you to sample the first plate. I've had to threaten Vincent and the other trolls with a butcher knife to keep them at bay. Come, come, quickly," she says, clapping her hands. "The other guests will be here any minute."

On the twelve-foot oak table in the dining room, a stunning display greets Liam: mushrooms stuffed with sausage, cream cheese under jalapeno jelly, assorted cheeses encircled with crackers, garlic bread dripping with butter, lox with tomatoes and onions, deviled eggs dusted with paprika, meatballs smothered with mushroom soup; salt-cured ham, deep-fried turkey, rare roast beef, cream of corn, assorted raw vegetables, steamed broccoli, cranberry sauce, sausage stuffing, and a collection of breads–circular loaves, baguettes, poppy-seed–beautiful food all. And in the middle of the gaudy display (beside the poinsettia centerpiece illumined by dozens of holiday candles) stand the opened bottles of wine that have fermented in Bob's own cellar. Liam surveys the entire spread, happy to feel a pang of real hunger again.

He is directed to sample certain dishes, the ones, Linda suggests with a hint of false modesty, she's not sure are edible. But every dish is delectable and she knows it. Liam groans in ecstasy after he samples each item and Linda smiles because an independent taster has confirmed what she knew in her heart all along. They slowly circle the table, sampling the fare; a deviled egg, a sliver of turkey with the crunchy crust, some garlic bread, a meatball awash in cream of mushroom gravy. Linda explains the history of each dish (where the recipe came from, what alterations have been made to it) and Liam eats and groans and nods, gesturing for more. Candles throw dancing light across the room.

By the time the other guests begin to trickle in, Liam is sated, at peace with the wine and the food that has settled within. Through the door and under the mistletoe come the bidden.

First, there's Joseph Hobart, a failed artist who makes his living teaching ceramics and painting to the spoiled progeny of the Denver elite. Bob's known him for years. The parents of Joseph's students–diamond-studded women and cashmere-coated men–tip him with liquor at Christmas so they can ignore him the rest of the year. The whining children and their blue-blood parents have no idea how Joseph fantasizes of dropping them all in a monstrous vat of cement, making living statues of the bored and the privileged in an attempt to capture the vacuity of their frivolous lives. He holds his bottle of Chivas Regal, watching his students climb into their Mercedes and Volvos, and wistfully thinks: *If only, if only I could find a vat big enough to fit them all. Wouldn't that be something? Then I would make a name as an artist, then the critics in New York would remember me.*

Then Bradford Fink scuffles through the door. Fink is a pony-tailed professor of literature at the local university who is trying to reconcile his label as a Marxian Feminist with the fact that he owns an upscale pool hall in lower downtown called the Artist's Loft. The establishment features polished hardwood floors, art from local students on its walls, and a clientele of twenty-something floozies who drink their micro-brewed beer while admiring the taut buttocks of lawyers, ad-men, and artistic wannabees as they bend over the pool tables around them. The business has made Bradford a wealthy and bitter man. He's become a cynic because America has finally lured him into her sweaty, capitalistic clutches and Marxists aren't supposed to clutch at all.

Then the rest of the invited arrive. Neighborhood friends, former Market employees, the Madman and his middle-aged date, widowed women, cousins of cousins, and then, Rebecca Kelly. The house is suddenly aflutter with eating, drinking, talking, laughing, and screeching. Liam sits in a red slay back chair in an alcove off the sitting room, drinking the bottle of wine at his feet, enjoying the fire at his elbow, watching the others. Though the other guests do now know it, Liam is writing without a pen. He thinks of how he'd describe the scene in words. What color of green is the holly? What shade of red the ribbons on the tree? In his mind, he assigns zingers to certain well-liked guests, while making others appear as fools. Dialogue is written. He gives each guest a history, imagines disappointments and heartaches, describing the sorrows and dreams that exist only in his head. He's over examining yet again, writing instead of living.

Watching Joseph Hobart nervously fidget with his collar, Liam imagines that his unease stems from a childhood Christmas wish that went unfulfilled. In a future story, Liam decides he will grant the man his wish, give him some physical object somehow capable of restoring hope. Then he eyes Bradford Fink with suspicion, distrusting his inch-long ponytail, deciding that he will be a pederast in a story not yet penned. No, not good enough, he decides, he'll be an *incestuous* pederast in some future tale, a man eventually jailed and thrown to the prison satyrs. Ah, the beauty of creation, Liam thinks with satisfaction, of placing people where you think they belong, of exercising authority over the chaos that swirls everywhere. He smiles and sips his wine, happy to feel the sense of ownership and control that has been so absent from his life these past eighteen months.

And in moments like this, my voice is completely overwhelmed by a cacophonous outburst from that friggin' frog. Yep, that's right, Little Napoleon is reborn. He's reborn in Liam's burning desire to control those around him, if only in his mind, if only in his prose. So, together, Liam and Little Napoleon sit among the guests at the party but are somehow detached from them, immune from the entanglements of personal relationships that eventually cause so much pain.

If someone were to ask Liam why he does not mingle with the others, Little Napoleon would whisper, *"Pourquoi, mon frere, a genius as towering as you, needs zum space to throw his thunder."* So Liam pushes the world away with words, distances himself with a pen. He hides behind an invisible sign that says, "Genius at Work. Do Not Disturb." It's much easier than being a man. However, no matter what Little Napoleon says, on some level Liam knows that a man adept at describing a life is often a man afraid to live one.

But Liam also knows that reality—whether embodied in an overweight golf caddy named Rudolph, an elderly handicapped woman named Mrs. Livingston, a black bus driver named Isaac, or a puerile store clerk named Madman—has a way of shattering the quiet and solitude a writer requires. Reality always trumps fiction. This realization hits home as Bob yanks Liam by his elbow and leads him toward the assembled clusters of guests.

"Come, my little scribe. Time to mingle."

They approach the Madman, Brad Fink, and Joseph Hobart as they talk and drink and surreptitiously survey the women at the party. Bob makes the introductions.

"Yes. Well. Bradford Fink, Liam McGarrity. Liam, Brad. Of course you know Eric Rodriguez, our self-dubbed 'Madman.' And this is Joseph Hobart, a dear friend from days and brain cells gone by. He's a painter by trade."

"Pleasure," Liam says, shaking their hands quickly.

"Yes. Well," Bob continues. "Dr. Fink is an old friend from the neighborhood, Liam, a professor of literature at UCD. Perhaps he can offer you some advice on your writing. And maybe later you can share with him your recent fascination with Whitman. Brad has become a successful entrepreneur of late, but he still dabbles in literature when he's not counting his money. Isn't that right, Brad?"

Fink nods and shakes Liam's hand, then stares at Bob. "Yes, Bob, I still dabble in literature, as you say. In fact, I'm the Graduate School Advisor in the department, moving up the food chain. But as far as Whitman, the Good Gray Poet, is concerned, all I can say is I hope your fascination with his work leaves you in time, Liam, like a virus of some sort." Fink looks to the ceiling as he speaks, playing with his ponytail with one hand, gesticulating with a glass of wine with the other. As he speaks, he winces, like what he must say causes him pain. "I find his work banal and bludgeoning, like he's beating the reader over the head with a blunt instrument. I prefer my literature precise and surgical, a bit more intellectual perhaps. Whitman's all blood and bone and flesh, too visceral, too physical for my tastes."

"Funny, that's what I like about him," Liam replies, suddenly angered. "I wanna book full of piss and vinegar, but like you say, it's just a matter of taste, I guess. I like Whitman, Henry Miller, and Thomas Wolfe. You probably prefer Henry James."

"Henry Miller?" the Madman asks, his eyes growing wide with the promise of debauched talk. "That's the porno guy, right Liam? The *Cancerous Topic*? I read some of his smut in junior high. Homeboy can get ya hard."

Liam looks at the Madman with incredulity while Bob pulls him from the group, trying to avoid a confrontation. (Since my death, Liam becomes angry because fools walk this earth with immunity, while others don't walk the earth at all.)

"Yes, Well," Bob responds over his shoulder as he leads Liam away. "There you have it then. A difference of opinion it seems, dissimilar notions of what and who is literary or pornographic. We'll pick this discussion up later. Gentlemen, if you'll excuse us…"

Bob takes Liam away by the elbow, leaving the Madman, Fink, and Hobart struggling for a suitable topic on which to converse. As they walk to a group of women, Bob pulls Liam close and begins to Bob-whisper in his ear. A Bob-whisper is what Liam would call an Irish whisper. It's louder than most full voices, peppered with giggles and "HA-HA's," and can be heard clearly from another room. A Bob-whisper is a futile whisper.

"Yes. Well," Bob begins, pulling Liam close. "Don't worry about those two. Fink is a cynic and Hobart is a drifter. You and I are neither. HA-HA! Away with us, to the women!" he says, flourishing his free arm. "After all, we're not eunuchs, we're men, and real men crave the soft caress of the finer sex. Look at them, son, like beautiful aromatic flowers awaiting the proper nose to appreciate their fragrance. Come. Let's cross into the mystery."

The women hear every word Bob says as he and Liam approach. All the women–save Bob's wife, Linda–smile and laugh in amazement at Bob's pronouncements. Bob winks at Liam, believing he has conveyed some secret masculine knowledge to this young Irish lad, when in fact he has notified the entire room that he plans on flirting with the four women beside the table. Rebecca Kelly is one of them.

"And here we are," Bob says as he stops Liam before the women. "You know Linda. And this is Sophia Francesca, a dear cousin of mine. Sophia, Liam. Liam, Sophia."

"Pleasure," Liam says, nodding.

"And this is Linda's sister, Grace. Notice the resemblance, young man, they're like two peas from the same twisted pod."

"Bob," Linda exclaims as she slaps him across the arm. "Don't be so damn obvious."

"Excuse me, my dear. As you know, it is my nature. And last but not least, Liam, you know Rebecca, our fair market damsel who never finds herself in distress. I believe this is the first time you've encountered each other in a social setting, yes? Rebecca, you look absolutely stunning," Bob continues. "The transformation you have undergone since work is amazing. Welcome to our humble abode. We are honored by your presence."

He performs a deep bow and kisses her hand, like he's welcoming a foreign dignitary.

"Thanks, Bob," Rebecca says as she pulls Bob to her and kisses him on the cheek. "I appreciate the invite. Good to see you too, Liam," she says as she turns to him. "You clean up pretty nice."

Completely self-assured, she leans over and kisses Liam lightly on the cheek. Liam is unnerved by her easy gesture and says nothing. She pulls back, looking him squarely in the eyes, and smiles. And, as if it had been planned, discussed, and agreed upon months before, the other women and Bob leave the two youngsters alone together. As the others walk away from him, Liam feels lost, like a drowning man searching for a life preserver. He looks to the other groups at the party–Fink and Hobart in the dining room, Dick-Tracy (who've just arrived) removing their yellow scarves in the foyer, Bob and Linda as they walk into the kitchen–trying to avoid this lovely woman's gaze, but it's no use, he feels her eyes upon him and is inevitably drawn back to her. I'm not even going to try and describe her to you because I'm not a writer and I'd never do her justice. Suffice to say, Liam can't resist her doe-like brown eyes, alabaster skin, and titian hair. She exudes a confident vulnerability, a strong surrender. Her smile grows wider and she is calm, patient, assured, like she'd be content to stand here staring at him for a year if that was what was required to get what she wants.

Hey, I know I'm dead and everything, but I just gotta say: the woman is a hottie. Not only is she physically striking, she's also on fire for the world. You can see it in her bold gaze, in her bursting brown eyes.

And as he looks at her for a few moments–the silence becoming less and less awkward, her smile assuring him somehow–Liam realizes that Little Napoleon, the past, his desire to injure, and his yearning to control everything under the sun, are lost somewhere between the folds of her flowered skirt as it gently flits about her legs. And just like that, on this ordinary solstice night at an extraordinary Denver house–with no celestial trumpets blaring, no sirens blazing, no sun brutally shining–things in my brother's life are again forever changed.

Rebecca takes Liam's hand, says, "C'mon," and leads him from the room. And though he doesn't know where she leads, for some reason the uncertainty doesn't bother him. The Madman spots them from across the room, shakes a fist high in the air, and yells, "You go, boy. You go." But Liam barely hears him. He's distracted by a familiar sensation that's been absent from his life for a while: a pang in his gut, a void that yearns to be filled again and again and again. He rubs his stomach as they walk, surprised he feels this way after all that he's eaten tonight, after all these months of desiring nothing from this physical world. Yep, it's true, for some reason, the kid's hungry again.

There will soon be no more priests. Their work is done . . .
A new order shall arise and they shall be the priests of man,
and every man shall be his own priest.
                                        –Walt Whitman

The Whiskey Priests
by
Liam McGarrity

Whitman said that whatever satisfies the soul is truth, but none of the explanations for Sean's death–Father Simpson's especially– satisfied my soul at all. He cornered me in the parking lot of St. Cecilia's an hour before the funeral.

"It's God's will, son," Simpson said as I looked up that still-towering church façade, wishing the distant stained-glass windows would somehow come alive with stories of solace. "He was too beautiful to be with us for long. Think how happy your mother is, up there with her son in heaven, laughing in the clouds, God and the angels and the saints all celebrating. What a party. Yes indeed, quite a bash. I know it's difficult, but His wisdom is infinite, Liam, he tests us so that we can see how strong we really are. You and I, son, are so very weak and small-sighted, but God does things for a reason, he has a plan for each of us. Patience, patience, patience. Time is the great healer."

But Father Simpson–this sandal-wearing son of a local car baron whose tan would make George Hamilton jealous–was about as spiritual as his father's best salesman and I didn't buy his explana-tion for a minute. I couldn't picture my brother and mother in the clouds playing harps and smiling down on the rest of us. I also couldn't imagine Sean coming back as a dog or dolphin, and knew there was no way he was burning in some pit with demons poking him with pitchforks. So after the priest left I stood alone behind the church, sipping some Tullamore Dew from a small flask, wondering where the hell he was. It was then I decided I couldn't accept the code of another–be it church, government, or prophet. I had to come to some kind of personal understanding because their explanations didn't satisfy my soul in the least.

As I pulled hard on the flask once again, I realized that I had no choice. I was compelled to become the first priest in a cosmology entirely of my own making. It was a priesthood I'd been bred and groomed for all my life. Suddenly, as the Tullamore Dew warmed my stomach, I heard the calling: I would become a whiskey priest.

* * *

The previous night I'd walked solemnly into the Falk house with a twelver of Coors in each hand, ceremoniously nodding in greeting to the assembled mourners. Benny was behind me with two bottles of Jameson. Each night a vigil was held to combat the hole, the emptiness each of us felt. At the vigils we ate ham sandwiches, watched the NBA playoffs, and told stories about Sean, trying to conjure him with our words. I'd close my eyes and listen to the stories and imagine him before me in whatever posture the storyteller described–then smile at the memory. But I'd open my eyes to find him gone, left only with a story, a memory, a mythology accreting around his absence.

It was as if each story we told was a piece of clay thrown on the outside of an indestructible glass orb that contained the empty space where Sean should have been. The clay stories accrued on the outside, caked one on the other, and though we told the stories to try to get closer to Sean, in reality each additional layer only pushed us farther and farther away from him. And with all that clay piling on all that glass, we couldn't see the space he should have occupied at all; it was covered with the stories. The more stories we told about him, the more distant and distorted he became. But whether the final result was a distancing from the real Sean or not, the words were the only things we had. We possessed no other tools. We were like a traveling collection of unarmed whiskey priests, searching for the words that might allow us to live with the hole in the middle of our fragile lives.

The previous vigils had been held at Deirdre's parents' house, my dad's place, and Kevin's. We needed another house for the last vigil, another venue in which to throw some clay, and the Falks' seemed like a logical selection. They lived in the same model house as the one in which I grew up, but on the next street over. They'd added a large family room off the back and–because their house was at the end of a cul-de-sac–they had a monstrous backyard. Tennis court, trampoline, horseshoe pit, basketball hoops, the whole bit. Large pine trees lined the back fence, protecting the backyard from the cars and their exhaust on Red Hill Ave.

Behind those trees, in the safety of the Falk backyard, another world existed; a world without cars, accidents, divorce, cancer, all the unpleasantness. As children, my brother, sisters, and I would play in that backyard for hours on end: a game of basketball, a few jumps on the trampoline, then some raucous runs down the Slip and Slide. The night before Sean's funeral even seemed idyllic there, like all the wars and disease and heartache were kept at bay by those trees, the walls of the living room, the power of the circle of people in that house. The Falk house was like a vestibule, the place where the priests go to prepare for the Mass, where they gather their wits in an attempt to make sense of the maddening world in which the rest of the congregation exists. We collected our vestments, our thoughts, the tools with which we had to face the abyss.

The living room served as the gathering place. Two golden couches together with a half dozen folding chairs, formed a jagged circle. Joe, Kevin, Aiko, Molly, and the rest of the mourners sat silently together. But every moment we stayed silent, that empty glass orb in the center of our circle expanded. As the scope of it increased we became cowed, frightened, like we too might disappear inside of it. We looked at the empty space in the middle of the chairs where Sean should've been, unsure what to do. Then Ursula Falk, a childhood friend of Sean's, asked me to tell the story about the whiskey-drinking episode at Sean's bachelor party six years before. I pulled some whiskey from Benny's bottle and began throwing some clay.

Benny, Stanley, and I were only sixteen years old and drove with Sean in his Mustang to Big Bear for the festivities. We sang songs along with the radio. "Think" by Aretha Franklin came on and we all screamed the words in unison. Sean shook the wheel playfully and before we knew it we were spinning in 360s on the ice, and Aretha said you better think about what you're trying to do to me and–as we saw the mountain, the snow, the trees, the road, then the space beyond the guardrail pass by our line of sight–we all looked at Sean and wondered what the hell he thought he was trying to do to *us*. Kill us I think.

But he regained control of the Mustang and we eventually arrived at the two-room cabin. Upon arrival, we were told there was a male initiation that had existed since the construction of the cabin in 1932. Of course they lied, there was no such ritual, but being sixteen we believed every word they said. At every bachelor party a bottle of whiskey (Jack Daniels in our case) was sent around a circle, they said, and each new initiate had to prove his manhood by imbibing. Kevin was the first to demonstrate this ritual. He tilted the Jack completely upside down and the gurgling bubbles in the closed end of the bottle was more than ample proof to my young friends and I that he was indeed guzzling whiskey. We looked at each other nervously, like maybe it would've been best if we'd gotten in that car crash, because the whiskey was gonna kill us anyway. Benny was the first of the virgins to tilt the bottle. He squinted and swallowed and then ran outside to leave his lunch in the snow. As he vomited over the balcony, Tom Boyle commented on the impressive speed with which the contents of Benny's stomach were disgorged.

"Nice distance, too, Benny, not bad for a young fella," he said.

As I watched the bottle being passed around our circle there at the Falk house, I thought of that day in the mountains and all the stories I've heard, written, or told that were either inspired by, connected with, or distorted through whiskey. Before too long the bottle was in my hands again. I thought of stories and whiskey, memory and its disappearance, holes and how we try to fill them.

Clay.

As the whiskey loosened our tongues, as the warmth from the spirits infiltrated our bellies, the stories became bigger than they should have been. The people began to become characters. Sean's smile beamed brighter, his stature expanded to Bunyanesque proportions, his life became gargantuan. We marveled at the beauty of the pieces of clay, distracted from the orb on which they rested. We found poignancy where before there had only been routine. Sean wasn't a simple man who worked hard and died tragically anymore. No, with each sensationalized story created by our whiskey-besotted memories, he became a legend, a hero of fiction whose death somehow dignified the living he left behind. And I realized that being a priest is simply telling the stories, relating the parables, providing the legends that enable the rest of the congregation to live with the holes in the middle of their lives.

Ursula asked me to tell some more stories, but I couldn't find the energy at that moment. I ran out of clay and couldn't understand why the rest of the group didn't mold their own pieces to throw. Standing up unsteadily, I walked to the backyard to get some air.

The Falks' trampoline was gone but the hole in the ground below it was still there. Grass grew through the cracks of the tennis court and the tattered vinyl net blew whimsically from the basketball rim. The pine trees weren't as tall as I remembered; they couldn't possibly keep all the unpleasantness at bay. All the things that I remembered were gone: the children, the sun, the trampoline, summertime basketball, the tennis net, Sean, the protection of the trees, and the immortality that seemed to accompany all those things.

I must've been dreaming for a while, because when I came back from that place in my mind where the dead people become fictional characters, Benny stood beside me with another whiskey. This one in a glass. Neat.

"Everybody's gone," he said.

"Funny, that's just what I was thinking," I responded.

"No, I mean inside. The others. They left."

"Even Molly?"

"Yeah, she thought you wanted to be alone, so she took off. She was dead."

"Yeah. I think we all are. What time is it, bro?"

"I don't know. A little after two maybe."

Benny and I drank our whiskeys and let the liquid and the warm night take us. We each looked at the empty backyard.

"What do you want to do now?" Benny asked.

I didn't know at first, then I thought and said, "I want to stay up all night drinking whiskey and telling stories to the emptiness, throwing clay at a hole that will never be filled." Benny looked at me askance, not sure what I meant. "I want to stay up all night so that tomorrow will never come, so that the day I bury my brother will never arrive, so that the funeral will never take place."

For a moment the crickets, those small couriers of solitude, were all that answered. Then some other answers pounded loudly in my ears: the memories hummed a small hymn to the invisible, the heavy darkness sang an elegy to its natural desire to conceal the unmanifest, and the oblique shadow world and its billions of ghosts whistled in my mind like a chorus of unnamable birds singing in a forest of their own making. I closed my eyes to hear the answers offered by all the naturally mute things. Then Benny put his hand on my shoulder and said:

"Tomorrows always come, Liam. And on some tomorrows– no, I'd say on most of them–you have to bury things. That's just part of it."

I laughed because I knew he was right. Then I put my hand on his and bowed my head in defeat to honor something I could not name, something that's never been seen or described very well, something always in the back of our minds, sometimes on the tip of our tongues. I bowed my head to honor something voiceless and divine. I conceded it all, because I knew that the sun would rise again and inaugurate the tomorrow that my brother would be planted in the ground like a seed. Tomorrows, receptacles of emptiness, the whiskey priesthood, the inexpressible, that damn sun. Everything seemed unavoidable.

* * *

The next morning–after I filled my flask and took a shot to steady myself–I showered and dressed unconsciously, like some-one else was doing it for me. I don't remember putting on deodor-ant, getting dressed, or brushing my teeth, but all those tasks were completed. Little Napoleon selected my wardrobe. Even though it was the day of my brother's funeral, he insisted the outfit was important. I wore a blue button-down shirt, tan pants, black leather belt, and black snakeskin cowboy boots that I'd purchased for the occasion. Say what I will about the little Corsican, I have to give him some credit; the sucker's got a wonderful feel for fashion.

The limousine took us to St. Cecilia's Church and I experienced the same nausea I felt when Sean and I used to go there as children. Deirdre took the kids inside to sit down and I stayed outside to greet people as they arrived. Kevin, Tom Boyle, Aiko, and a few others stood uneasily around the hearse. We complimented each other on the clothes our respective Little Napoleons had picked out for us. We talked uneasily, unsure what to do next, uncomfortable in our collared shirts and dress shoes. We fidgeted, not being our own priests at all. We were only pallbearers, men preparing to carry a corpse.

A little aside. In ancient times a pall was a rich robe worn by a king at his coronation. Picture it: The bedraggled subjects of the kingdom lining a road under a sun-splashed sky, the music of golden trumpets echoing down pristine canyons, and the purple ermine flowing off the shoulders of the king-to-be as he walks down the aisle beneath the trumpets and the admiring gaze of his people. The pallbearers were those who solemnly walked behind the king, holding his lush garment so that it wouldn't be soiled by the maculate world. But by the time of the Roman Empire, the definition of a pall had dramatically changed. For some reason, pall was used to describe the cloth that was draped over a chalice or a coffin. Eventually a pall became anything dark or gloomy that was spread over something. Like the black smoke from the fire was a pall on the land. So according to that definition, Kevin, Aiko, and the rest of us, were preparing to carry something dark and solemn into that church, nothing majestic at all.

Personally, I prefer the original definition. So the day of Sean's funeral, we pallbearers weren't about to carry something hideous or dark. No, the coffin was simply the beautiful garment of a king-in-wait, the ceremonial robe for a distant coronation. So we should have celebrated and the wine and whiskey should've flowed, not because we wanted to forget, but because–like those peasants so many centuries before–we wanted to celebrate the promotion of one of our humble own. And the women should have shown their brown midriffs in tribute, their tan calves trembling tightly in the sun, the men should've worn running shoes to aid their attempt in chasing the king, my brother, to wherever he went, and the children should have sung celebratory hymns at the top of their lungs. And all of us should've gone to the beach together in the presence of the elements: the water, the sun, the clouds, the sand, the wind, and the people should've danced, *the people should have fuckin' danced!*

But none of us knew the real definition of pall at the time, so the women wore black concealing dresses that constricted their bodies, their hair tied tautly in buns atop their heads; the men shuffled awkwardly in their stiff shoes, the unfamiliar ties restricting the flow of air to their lungs. They filled the church. And we pallbearers were unsure in our budding priesthood, waiting for someone to tell us what to do.

* * *

Mr. Wheeler, the Bereavement Advisor from Green's Mortuary, was there for that very purpose. Nobody complimented him on his appearance (his Little Napoleon sucked) because he wore a light blue polyester suit and a plain brown tie that barely reached below his concave chest. He stood a bit over five foot eight but if you asked him his height he'd tell you he was almost six foot. The lubricant in his sandy blonde hair caught the sun at various times, glistening orange then blue, like an oil stain on a driveway. The look of feigned concern he wore had been perfected by years of practice. He shook his head periodically to signify that he couldn't believe Sean was dead either. His ebony eyes darted around in their sockets like he was a nocturnal rodent thrown from his hole after an extended period in the dark. He smelled of cigarette smoke and cheap cologne and constantly clapped his yellowed hands like we were all about to go somewhere together. In reality he was just anxious to get Sean underground so that he could return to the funereal, shadowy world behind the doors of Green's Mortuary.

Deirdre and I had ventured into that shadowy world a few days before. When we opened the door to the mortuary, the prerecorded organ music of a memorial service greeted us. We quietly walked to Wheeler's office door and knocked lightly. "Come in," a tremulous voice answered from beyond. Behind the door was an ornate antique desk with a small lamp atop it. The green lampshade threw a ghostly-green pallor over the desk. Shadows enveloped the rest of the room and I saw the dark outline of an obscure painting on the far wall. Wheeler sat behind the desk solemnly and patiently, like he'd been expecting us for days and would gladly wait some more if it was required. His face appeared from the dark like a greenish-white mask floating in the darkness, a disembodied mouthpiece from a world most of us would like to ignore.

"I'm Liam McGarrity, I called earlier…about my brother, Sean," I began, sitting down in one of the plush leather chairs in front of the desk. "This is Deirdre, my brother's wife…the widow."

Deirdre stifled a sniffle with a tissue and sat beside me.

"Yes," Wheeler responded, his bony fingers intertwined piously before him. "Of course my deepest sympathies go out to you both. Mrs. McGarrity, I know this is especially difficult for you. We'll try to make this as easy as possible. I know it's unpleasant business, the selection of the burial vessel, but it *is* important. With this purchase you say so many things: how much you loved the decedent, what type of man he was, what you believe the hereafter will provide. And, it is the last thing on this earth, the final material object you can purchase for the dearly departed. A gift to your husband, so to speak."

After his opening salvo he stood up slowly. It was only then I realized how small he was. The monstrous desk with the intricate carvings in the legs and detailed moldings on its sides, came nearly to his chest. He turned his back and walked away, disappearing into the dark like a ghoul. From the darkness his voice rose ominously.

"Yes, Mr. And Mrs. McGarrity, I can remember when my beloved grandfather passed away in Missouri, lo those many years ago, and my grandmother had a crypt built especially for him. Seraphim and cherubim, the trumpets of the angels, granite, marble, no expense was spared. Magnificent, truly a magnificent tribute. And when my father said to her, 'It's too much mother, too much,' she simply said, 'Nothing's too much for your father.' Yes sir, I'll never forget that: wise words from a wise woman. So I say to you both now, in this time of terrible trouble, it's always better to err on the side of plenty than on the side of want. You don't want to regret anything once the interment has been completed. After all, we only pass once. So, if you come with me to the showroom, we'll get started on the selection process."

And he quickly reappeared from the darkness, his face once again ghoulishly illumined by the lamp on his desk. Deirdre stopped him in his tracks with a voice surprisingly strong.

"Mr. Wheeler. With all due respect, my husband was a carpenter; a simple man with strong, simple desires. Ornament is not our concern. And we plan on honoring his life in ways beyond the material, so we would like a plain wooden box. Nothing more. Sean didn't know wealth, refinement, or plenitude in life, so he sure as hell doesn't need it now. In fact, the cruder the better; something uneven, with evidence that it took some violence to create it; sap, splinters, uneven lines. I want the coffin to match my husband–" she said, suddenly sapped of her strength, her eyes brimming with tears. "Yes, the coffin should reflect the man it carries, so I want a plain wooden box–beautiful in its simplicity, enchanting in its complete lack of artifice. We don't want to betray him now."

Then she began to weep. Since Sean's death this would happen periodically. She would alternate between periods of dazed reverie, forced gallows humor, and uncontrollable weeping. It was like she just heard about the death twenty to thirty times a day. Wheeler nodded his head like he understood her desires perfectly, and walked ahead of us to the showroom.

Of course, he had no such coffin on his premises. After all, you can't purchase Cadillac hearses, beautiful buildings in North Tryon, and imported French desks with the proceeds from *those* kinds of coffins, so Wheeler simply ignored Deirdre's requests and opened the doors to the showroom. He bowed and said:

"Well, Mrs. McGarrity, we don't have anything like that *per se*, but I think you'll find the Aspen Enchantment model to your liking. It's hand-crafted oak with a lovely varnish and should suit your needs just fine. And at just 4,200 dollars, it's quite a bargain as well."

This same man was now instructing me and the other pallbearers as to our duties and assignments for the funeral. I hated him.

"You stand at the front left, Liam, and as soon as the bagpiper begins you should start walking…"

With each direction, admonishment, and utterance from

Wheeler's small, ferret-like mouth, I grew more and more angry, felt a bit more cheated. Because it wasn't enough that he had to sell us a coffin we didn't want at a price nobody should pay; it wasn't enough he kept Sean's body hidden behind his locked refrigerator doors or that he drove Sean around in an expensive Cadillac he would never ride in while alive. No, it was that he acted like it was *his* funeral to run, *his* day and not ours.

As we picked up the coffin in preparation for our entrance to the church, Wheeler said, "Be careful now, be careful. Don't scratch it on the doorjamb."

And as I picked up my corner of that too-perfect coffin, listening to Wheeler for the last time, I thought again of all the opportunities that I'd missed in the days since Sean's death, all the things I should've done.

I should've snuck into the San Bernardino County Morgue in the middle of the night and stolen Sean's body (like Gram Parsons's buddies did), and taken it to the desert and burned it in a sacrifice to some one or thing I wish would show itself. I at least should've taken his body to my dad's house and preserved him myself somehow. Laid his body out in a box on two sawhorses made from his own two hands. I should've set up a food buffet right near his body and had a *real* Irish wake. Ham and Sean, the corpses of a pig and a man right next to each other. I should've played loud music and invited friends to wrestle in the living room; Sean laid out right near the match like some stoic referee. I should've lit candles and placed them on the sawhorses and the shadows would've grown large on the wall like flitting ghosts come to pay their last respects.

I should've invited Frank Paloma, the ranger from Sad Shepherd Campground, and sung "Finnegan's Wake" with him at the top of my lungs–half-empty whiskey bottles in both our hands, loosened ties around our necks, sweat-stained shirts stuck to our chiseled frames. In that song some Irishmen throw a wake for a guy with whiskey and porter. A bit of the whiskey spills on the corpse and revives Finnegan, brings him back from the dead. Most Irishman believe in the rejuvenative power of the *uiscebeatha*, the *eau de vivre*, which if given the chance whiskey can accomplish anything, even the resurrection of the dead. Frank and I should've drunkenly swayed with our arms on each other's shoulders as we sang, staggering and spilling some whiskey on Sean's corpse, giving him a reason to join the living again. Come on, Seanny, get up and scream:

"Thunderin' Jesus, do you think I'm dead?"

I should've built his coffin myself; my hands bloodied and calloused, the splinters from the burial vessel festering under my skin as a reminder. I should've climbed the fence of the graveyard at midnight with a shovel and a six-pack (beneath the moon and the clouds and the stars) and dug his grave myself–because burying bodies has a little to do with putting bodies underground, but a lot more to do with ownership, with being your own priest.

In other words, I should've done something to claim the day I buried my brother as the single most important thing to ever happen to me, but I didn't. I was letting other people be the priests, letting others tell me what to do. Wheeler's admonishments concerning his precious box made it clear to me that I'd wasted my opportunity. I wanted to kill him.

So I dropped my corner of the coffin and went after him. The remaining pallbearers' shoulders strained under the imbalance my absence created. I chased Wheeler around the casket and then around the hearse, and some of the mourners in the back row heard a little ruckus and turned to watch. Because the soles of my boots were slick, it was difficult to change directions and I slipped on the asphalt and had to catch myself on the turn. Wheeler must have been about forty-five years old but he was small and wiry and damn quick for his age. He'd probably been chased a lot of times. My efforts were all for naught because Wheeler made it to the passenger side of the hearse, dove in frantically, and quickly locked the doors. As he breathed heavily and sculpted his hair back into place with his bony hand, I saw his nose flit back and forth like a rodent trying to sense the danger in the wind.

I pointed at him through the smoky tint windows and said, "If you say another word, I'm going to fuckin' kill you! So help me God, you son of a bitch, I will kill you."

I too caught my breath and looked back over my shoulder at the other pallbearers and the concerned onlookers in the back of the church. The other pallbearers had set the coffin down on the pavement of the St. Cecilia's parking lot and I realized as I saw them smiling and then laughing out loud, that the simple act of chasing a small, poorly-suited man around a hearse had somehow galvanized us, made us feel like we were taking control of this day again. I approached the other pallbearers and leaned on the coffin with them. Together, with the whiskey on our breath and the king-to-be beneath us, we enjoyed one last laugh together with Sean. After a few moments Aiko said, "Let's go," and we carried my brother into the church with purpose, like we were priests who knew what we were doing. We smiled across the casket at one another with the dead weight in our hands, and strode into the world of the old priests, unsure of what lay before us.

* * *

Of course, St. Cecilia's austere wood pews, story-less stained-glass windows, and English-impaired priest were what lay before us. As we carried Sean into the church, I noticed Father Francois Nguyen standing piously behind Father Simpson on the altar and thought that he'd aged rather well. Certainly, he'd gained a few pounds and sprouted a few dozen gray hairs, but otherwise he was unchanged from the man I knew twelve years before. The walls of the Church had preserved him nicely.

We carried Sean to the stand in front of the altar and the priest blessed the casket with holy water. Women wept, babies cried, a bagpiper played. Flowers enveloped the altar, their redolence masked by the incense thickly hovering in the chill church air. The pallbearers dispersed and found their respective seats.

I sat in the front row. Erin, Sean's youngest daughter, sat on my lap, fidgeting from side to side, anxious to venture beyond the domain of the priests, yearning to go outside, like her father. Her sister Brigid sat beside Deirdre, looking vacantly off into the distance like she was somewhere else entirely. I looked around at the whispering crowd and congratulated Sean on a fine turnout. People spilled out of the doors in back, others leaned against the walls in the aisles, directly under those giant speakers that would soon screech with the feedback of Father Simpson's speech. Some men looked at their stiff shoes uneasily, others held their daughters' hands a little tighter than usual. Several well-dressed women looked sideways at their husbands and wondered how much they'd miss them if they were to die on the morrow.

Father Simpson began to speak, hoping to answer some of the unvoiced questions the yearning faces of the congregation asked. But of course the dated speakers distorted his voice into incomprehensible oblivion. And because the sections of the Mass–the welcome, the first and second readings, the meaningless ritualistic chants offered in response to vague, meaningless questions–were so familiar to me, I was able to drown them out and focus on Father Simpson, the man who kicked Sean out of Aquinas High School all those years before. He had Art Garfunkel hair, wore Birkenstock sandals, and a puzzled expression, like he too didn't know if what he said was true. His voice was weak, cracking; his heart didn't seem to be in it.

And as I think back to Father Simpson–that priest from the old order–I think about Rebecca Kelly and Walt's priest theory again. Every man and woman their own priest, responsible for their own salvation, listening to some voice of eternity that speaks from within each one of us. I'm not talking about listening to Little Napoleon, the voice concerned only with the transient; I'm talking about the voice that rises in his absence. The voice that we so often stifle, forget, or ignore because that's easier than taking a chance on believing that what we desire, what our consciences tell us to be true, should dictate how we behave. If only each of us could kill our dictators and listen to that other voice, the one aching to return to the Source, aching to liberate us from our petty concern for self.

As I looked at the crumpled paper that held the eulogy I'd written with my own hand, my own pen, my own glass of whiskey by my side, I thought it might be the beginning of my priesthood; a faltering, inconsistent, whiskey-inspired priesthood, but an individual priesthood nonetheless. Maybe Sean's death wasn't an ending of his life so much as the beginning of mine, I thought. I tried to make myself believe, tried to listen to that other voice, but the voice of Father Simpson kept on intruding. And everybody knelt when he bid them, stood when he asked, spoke when he ordered. I cursed myself as I obeyed his commands because I wanted to be my own priest, but it's so damn hard. We've all grown so accustomed to ignoring the most ennobling parts of our selves, grown so used to listening to what other priests, teachers, and politicians have told us that we've forgotten that kingdoms and Gods are within us.

Then the time for my eulogy arrived and I had to confront that ocean of faces. Standing at the pulpit, I felt like I was at the prow of a ship. The faceless people below were like separate drops of water in an interminable ocean. My feet were unsteady because I'd grown accustomed to the predictability of the dry land. The mist billowing from the bow of the ship sprayed my face, inhibiting my sight. I blinked quickly just trying to see the paper on the pulpit before me. Then I looked past the people to the distance and fought to see Sean, but couldn't see past the next wave swelling ahead and the spray its crash engendered. I wanted the waves to stop so that I could see the horizon again, to gain some perspective, but the air turned gray and the rain came and I looked at the paper in my hands and it was sopped, unreadable again. The ink bled over the page, my knees shook, the sea air choked my breath, and I kicked in the water, trying to stay afloat.

Waves and small heavy words, the ocean and a drowning man.

The waves rose and broke over my head, the storm seeming to rage against me and me alone. I swallowed the seawater, choking and gasping, the church like a lost, captain-less ship. Everyone else in St. Cecilia's was dry and I knew then that some people never see the storms around them, never understand how directionless their paths really are. Couldn't they see how small they were, how absolutely paltry their lives were in the face of those waves? Didn't their stomachs revolt at the size of the ocean, the fragility of their vessel? I screamed at them to look, listen, *see*, how important Sean's life was, but my voice was lost beneath mountains of waves. The wider my mouth opened, the more seawater I took on, the more my message was lost. And it was the first time I realized how futile words can be against the forces with which we're bombarded, the waves from the sea whose source lies beyond any means of our myopic reckoning.

Then as I looked at Father Simpson–the sandal-wearing reciter of a script whose message has long since lost its relevance–nodding off in his chair beside me, I thought the old priests weren't dying quick enough. I wanted to kill him, destroy the intermediaries between ourselves and the storms. Then I studied the casket at my side and wanted to steal Sean's body and throw it over my shoulder and get him away from that church, take him down a road only he and I would appreciate. Then, as the pulpit teetered and swooned, as the water from the ocean blinded my eyes, I yearned to stop all the rain from falling, all the waves from rising and threatening this broken ark.

I wanted…

I wanted…

I wanted …

I wanted to fuckin' scream!

But instead, I did nothing but talk. My gestures and speech lost in the sea below me, forgotten in the heart of a storm. I slouched back to my seat with the roar of the ocean still in my ears and realized that being your own priest means you have to see the storm and understand your impotence against it. Still, you've got to find a way to speak. You must mumble your inarticulate message–the one inspired by the unfathomable mystery–at the next wave as you see it approach. The message is found in your heart, the place that tries to connect your feeble flesh with something that lasts, the place you wish was large enough to contain what has never been embodied in a single being: death and timelessness, desire and peace. Priests get ripped to pieces by the impossible conundrum.

And as if all that wasn't enough, there's one more thing–when you're a true priest, you've got to love the people who forget your impassioned words.

* * *

The great thing about being a whiskey priest as opposed to the Catholic kind, is that when you grow despondent that nobody understands what you're talking about, when a storm knocks you flat on your ass in the middle of a morbid church, you don't have to go in search of a little boy to distract you from the mystery that's impossible to encapsulate with words. You've got the whiskey instead. Although I didn't get another whiskey until after the burial, the wait was more than worth it. After we planted Sean in the ground, we had a party at Deirdre's parents' house because everybody knows that the only difference between an Irish funeral and an Irish wedding is one less drunken Irishman.

Sean and Deirdre's shotgun wedding reception had taken place at Deirdre's parents' house only six years before. When I walked through the door the day of the wedding, Sean's friend Jed stood in the entryway pouring champagne into plastic cups for the guests as they entered, slugging an occasional mouthful for himself. The day of the wake, however, Jed poured shots of whiskey for the mourners, the latter occasion calling for stronger medicine. He carried a bottle of Bushmills in one hand and a shot glass in the other. While most of the others wore dark suits and spoke in hushed tones, Jed wore faded jeans and a denim shirt and spoke in a party voice, like he was trying to convince everybody that it was okay that Sean was dead. His long brown hair had not been combed; his old brown shoes had never been shined. Jed was a talented musician, but money in an open guitar case was often his only income. Women fell in love with him when he sang old Jim Croce songs, then grew tired of him because he never once thought of marriage or buying a house.

Sean met Jed when they were both working at a youth camp in the mountains outside Lake Arrowhead. Sean was the wrangler, Jed the entertainment. Jed looked like the picture of Jesus I'd seen at First Communion class when I was young, the one where Jesus looked like an emaciated hippie with teary-blue, sympathetic eyes. To look in those eyes was to believe in the therapeutic value of whiskey, the unassailable genius of John Lennon, or the feasibility of a petroleum-free world. That is to say, looking in Jed's eyes was enough to make you believe in anything. But as I watched him from a distance the day of the funeral, I realized he was no prophet or savior, he was just a charismatic man, maybe a whiskey priest, trying to make everybody believe that it was indeed a party and not a wake. He had the right idea, I thought, but it seemed like he was trying to convince himself more than anybody else.

Approaching complete strangers with a smile and a wink, Jed poured a shot for them then one for himself. Some shook their heads and haughtily refused, some looked around to ensure their wives were not watching, then quickly downed their drinks with a wince. I leaned in the doorway between the patio and the living room, a ham sandwich in my right hand, and laughed. Though I'd not yet spoken to Jed that day, I felt closer to him than any of the others. At least he was trying to be his own priest, trying to hear what the voice within his chest wanted him to do. Jed was definitely a member of that army of rebels whose number had recently been reduced by one.

He approached another member of that army, Benny, as if the dreadlocks falling past his shoulders were the custom epaulets of his rebellious rank. "You'll have a whiskey with me, won't you partner?" Jed asked.

"I sure as hell will," Benny responded.

"Good," Jed continued as he poured the Bushmills from the bottle. "Sean would've wanted it that way." He clinked Benny's glass with his bottle and they both imbibed heartily. Then he retrieved the glass from Benny and walked quickly to the kitchen like a soiled clown trying to spread a little joy.

I ate my ham sandwich in the doorway and watched the others.

In the family room to the left, a few mourners assembled. Joseph, a cousin from Buffalo, held Nora's baby on the couch. Dapper as always with his Armani suit, gold watch, and Italian shoes, Joseph sat with a bewildered expression on his face, like he'd just witnessed a horrible car accident he could neither understand nor prevent. The accident unwound before his mind's eye time after time. He could not look away, could not stop the scene from playing again and again. Occasionally, when he pictured Sean dying there on the dirt, he winced like he'd been punched by an invisible Opponent, like a rib or a collarbone was broken by the blow. He looked at the baby, shook his head, then gazed unseeingly off into the distance, nursing the new break. Like a broken collarbone or a broken rib, Joseph's injury was not obvious to the naked eye. He had no physical bruises, no black eyes, no crutches. I only got glimpses of the pain the break caused when Joseph grimaced or shook his head from side to side. Each painful wince was like a broken bone poking through his skin, and Joseph could no longer imagine his life without his new break, his new gash, his new Opponent. And he thought: *The break will never heal because the Opponent will never stop punching me. I've just got to learn how to walk with the jagged break poking at my guts.* But he knew: *I'll never be the same.*

He looked into the baby's eyes then up into mine. And in the instant that his gaze met mine from across the room, I saw something I'd never seen before. As his weak smile beamed and the disbelief and tears brimmed in his eyes, I saw that there's a certain beauty in the faces of those with the internal breaks. And no matter how beautiful their clothes, how well-groomed their appearance, this broken man's beauty simply cannot be concealed. I can't describe this broken beauty very well because it doesn't last long enough to properly study it. All I know is that most people try to hide their wounds because they think the defeat that begets their broken beauty is a disgrace. Most don't want to admit to themselves that the Opponent beat them; they don't want others to know they have bones that break. When their gazes meet another's, they turn away because they're embarrassed by the vulnerability to which their faces give witness.

But no matter what they do, no matter how they try to conceal it, at the strangest moments they feel the break again, because the Opponent always finds the spot where the old fracture is and punches it again and again and again. And when you or me or Joseph feel that old break snapping anew, there is nothing to do but accept that the Opponent will be kicking our ass forever. We will always lose that fight.

So Joseph sat with the baby on the couch: confused, in pieces, the break painfully apparent in his brimming eyes and tremulous smile. I watched him there and, in a flash, saw the beauty of a man shattered by the Opponent, a man grimacing for himself but still hoping this baby's life might be long and filled with hours of striving. And I thought of something Yeats said. That nothing can be sole or whole that has not been rent asunder first. I too understood that only a broken man can ever hope to be complete. It's difficult to explain, but a broken man becomes stronger in the damaged parts although he's punched there continually. It seems we've got to be ripped to pieces, suffer break after break after break, before we can be properly constructed again. We must become fractured and hideous if we ever hope to achieve any degree of beauty.

* * *

Inside the house, the proceedings continued. Old waddling women in pearls and polka-dotted dresses hovered near the food table in the dining room, talking, picking food from plates, refilling glasses, and replacing empty platters of ham. Young boys ran through the house, shirts untucked, dress trousers soiled, and were chastised by aunts and mothers who exclaimed, "Slow down, lads, for Chrissake, slow down." Young girls sat daintily on folding chairs, cake-filled paper plates on their laps, short legs slowly swinging below them. A few men stood in the kitchen, one hand wrapped around a Guinness bottle or a Budweiser can, one hand jingling loose change in an otherwise empty pocket. Several men played darts in the garage, not wanting to stray too far from the brimming coolers of beer that fed them there.

Jed flitted from room to room, pouring shots of Bushmills, clinking glasses, saying, "Sean would've wanted it that way."

Molly and Nora stood in the kitchen and nodded vacantly at the advice and consolations offered by the Women from the Homeland. With an upturned red nose, faded auburn hair, and glass of Brandy-spiked punch in her hand, an old woman said, "It's a long road that has no turning, Nora. The most interesting roads are filled with hills, detours, bandits, and banshees. And the Irish *always* walk the roads with the most turns in them. Wait 'til yer our age, lass, when the weight and curves of the road have bent your back, sucked your teats dry, and gnarled your fingers."

Another said to Molly, "Ahh, Molly, 'tis the same with all of us. We've got the luck o' the Irish. All bad."

Hours passed, bottles clinked in trashcans, and voices rose as drinks fell. Whiskey priests were being born every minute. And outside, most of the Men from the Homeland, my father included, assembled.

"Christ, Sean," one of the men said to my father as he put his hand on his shoulder. "From Cromwell to Black '47, it's been the same. If it's not an informer giving up Michael Collins, it's the Black and Tans shooting our innocent. Yes sir, Sean, God gives the Irish the worst because they're the only race on earth that can handle all the trouble. But, praised be, He also gave us the whiskey. Not to console us, mind you, but to keep us from ruling the world!" He laughed and pulled my dad closer. "Seriously Sean, they say thirst is the end of drinking and sorrow the end of drunkenness, but we can't help ourselves, the love of the whiskey is a part of us all." And as he finished his supposed consolation and saw that his glass had miraculously been refilled, he said, "Anyway, Sean, may you be a half an hour in heaven before the devil knows you're dead!"

Then he laughed, raised a spilling glass of John Powers, drank, and began to clap along with my cousin Francis's mandolin as he played "Black and Tans." While my father drifted to the side yard to smoke and ruminate, an inebriated crowd gathered around Francis's chair. The Men from the Homeland nodded aggressively with the music, like every word he sang was the verification in verse of the message that had been written in their hearts by some long ago pen. They beat their feet in time and clapped along with the guitar. Red running noses, yellowish bloodshot eyes, white socks with dark dress slacks, they clapped and sang and shook their heads at the way the world had treated them. They were Irishmen cursing their bad luck yet again, like they themselves had nothing to do with the foolhardy revolutions, tragic evictions, and drunken defeats that were so much a part of the stories they told, the songs they sang, and the maxims that so powerfully governed their lives.

For better or worse, I am one of them.

I'm certain I'm one of them because the last thing I remember (before passing out face first into the bathroom mirror three hours later) was a scene in which self-pity, whiskey, and tragic memories were prominent. Just before I lost consciousness, I watched Jed studying a picture on the wall that led to the hallway bathroom. In the picture, Sean and Deirdre held each other in front of the cliff on which they were married in Laguna Beach. A garden of sunflowers stood before them and behind the railing the cactus native to that coast squatted. The groomsmen spread beside them like human wings and wore sunglasses to fight the glare. The wind played haphazardly with our hair and ties. The Pacific rolled against the rocks behind us, carrying packets of late afternoon sunlight to the shore on each of its crests. Even in the picture, the sun was almost too bright to face.

Jed stared at the picture dazedly; one hand on the wall, his nose almost pressed to the glass of the frame, like if he got close enough the picture might become reality. His Bushmills was almost gone but he clung to the neck of the bottle like a drowning man to a life preserver. With no shot glass in the other hand, I knew he'd given up even the appearance of moderation. He strained his eyes and moved even closer to the picture, like he wanted to go back to the time captured there. Then he shook his head and took another drink. He no longer acted like he was a clown at a party; he acted like he wanted to get drunk and forget. The whiskey on his tongue and the image of Sean, Deirdre, and the rest of us on the wall before him, together made him grimace and contort his face. He thought:

When did all this happen? I was just pouring him a glass of champagne. When did this picture become a relic? When did Sean become a memory, a ghost captured in a photo?

Jed's eyes shone like glass razors and he wasn't smiling anymore. I don't know, my drunkenness could've projected itself, the dampness in my own eyes could've fooled me, but I swear it looked like he was crying. So–through my foggy alcoholic prison–I yelled to him, "Hey Jed! Sean would've wanted it that way!"

My slurred voice surprised him momentarily, then he turned his head and drunkenly smiled at me, his eyes beginning to droop and accept the inevitable. He raised the bottle toward me as an offering to the picture on the wall in front of him and I gave him one of Sean's crooked thumbs-ups in response. And then I thought of all the liquids in the past two days: the Tullamore Dew, the Guinness, the Bushmills, the waves in the church, the tears I saw forming in all of our eyes. I knew then that Jed and I were both just whiskey priests trying to find our voices. And as the unshed tears glistened in Jed's eyes, I realized that tears are often like wishes. Sometimes they go unfulfilled.

And my cousin Francis, another whiskey priest, played melancholy rebel songs in the dark backyard, a half-empty bottle of John Powers on the ground beside him. Everybody else had gone. He was singing to himself with his eyes closed, alone with his song and his whiskey, alone with his blessings and his lack. Like a crow suspended in a nighttime sky.

Like a blind man.

SIX

I know I've been a little rough on the scholars, guys like my bro who sit around with their noses stuck in books half their lives: reading, writing, pondering the great questions. Here's my complaint with the world of books: no matter what teachers, editors, or librarians might say, writing's all in your head, intangible, like the friggin' air. It's just the inadequate expression of things that exist solely in the mind, things you can't actually touch. I don't care if it's a history book, biography, even a collection of photographs. None of it's real. The stuff between the covers might give you a glimpse of reality, a peek at something you've not yet seen, but it can't hold a candle to reality itself. Never could. I mean, who ever read a description of a man riding a horse that ever approached the sensation of actually riding that horse? Who ever read about a man and woman's first dance that could rival the dance itself? Nobody, that's who. Joyce, Faulkner, and Shakespeare never even had *that* kind of talent. Don't get me wrong; I'm not saying that reading and writing are worthless. Hey, even *I* understand that writing can open your eyes to the world outside, maybe give you some insights on what it means to be a part of this powerful play. All I'm saying is that writing is a pale substitute for the ride, a paltry excuse not to dance.

As he sits before the fire with Rebecca, Liam is finally beginning to vaguely sense that. He's confused, though, caught between the intangible world expressed in his writing and the physical world of which he and this beautiful woman are now a part. It's only now that he's beginning to see that this ordinary conversation is more colorful and loaded with meaning than the most sacred story or

151

poem, including *Leaves of Grass*, including anything he's ever written. And it's a revelation to him. It's taken the poetry of Walt Whitman, eighteen months of brooding, the presence of a dead brother, and a high-spirited woman to make Liam finally understand that–since last May 16th–he's been more dead than me. But now he can't get enough of this woman before him. As he sits staring at her, the fire warm on his arm, he feels that if he catches up on Rebecca's life, he'll catch up with the world.

Rebecca tells Liam that she is the fifth of a six-child family of Kansas Catholics. Her grandfather was a painter of some note in Buena Vista, Colorado, until he was killed by an unknown assailant who painted the word "COMMUNIST" on his cabin door after he finished slitting his throat. When Rebecca turned eighteen, a month or so after her high school graduation, she moved from Ellsworth, Kansas with her older brother, Lex, to live in the place her grandpa had vacated. In a rusted Ford pickup, they drove to their grandfather's cabin where they made a simple life for themselves. Lex worked construction when the weather allowed, plowed snow and did handyman work when it didn't. She worked at a local market in the winter and on the Arkansas River as a whitewater guide in the summer.

Her grandpa (a man who insisted everyone call him Sparky, even though his name was James Michael Curley) was a bibliophile so she and her brother would build a fire after their days were done and read until midnight or so from a library of over three thousand titles. From Herodotus and Josephus to Ken Kesey and Cormac McCarthy, she read, not knowing what she would read next until she finished the one in her hands. Books on Japanese watercolor artists, women troubadours, U.S. history prior to 1492, the original notes of the explorers of the fifteenth and sixteenth centuries, the Koran, the Bible, the Bhagavad Gita, the Upanishads, Joyce, Dickens, Faulkner, Hesse, Giono, Cendrars, Kazantzakis, William Kennedy, Novalis, Jim Morrison, Kerouac, Rimbaud, and the single volume she kept coming back to again and again and again. The volume of *Leaves of Grass* that now rests on Liam's table at home.

Lex chased a bad woman to Denver only to be dumped in favor of a CSU frat boy shortly after arriving. Rebecca followed a few months ago to comfort him, just biding her time until the winter snow melted and filled her river with its sometimes destructive and treacherous waters. She often talks like that: the Arkansas—with its hulking shoulders bursting through the Southern Colorado canyons— is *her* river, the towering Collegiate Peaks *her* mountains.

Because her blood warms with each passing day, she knows she must go soon. She can't stay inside so she walks for hours after work trying to tire her blood out, trying to make the anxiousness vanish. Although the cabin is hundreds of miles away from where she and Liam now sit, she says the books, the trees, the wildflowers (White Locos are her favorite), the cool water from the top of the world (in July, she says, even though the temperature of the air is in the nineties, the water is so brisk it still takes your breath away), the pasture that rolls at the feet of the mountains like a dog curled up at its master's feet—all call to her. She won't be able to fight them much longer. She will go soon, she says. She has no choice.

"I listen to the wind, the sun, the blood," she tells him.

She exists in a place so different from the one Liam has inhabited for the past eighteen months. A place that has no time for pathos, fear, or over-analysis. An elemental place. The snow falls, stays a few months, and the animals and the plants lie in a state of dormancy, dead for a time. Then the earth changes its place in relation to the sun and the snow melts, the rivers swell, things grow again and the living things wake up and yearn to go outside, their time for death now through. Similarly, Rebecca's grandfather was born, grew up, created art, touched many lives, then died. She's not bitter about the way he was killed. It doesn't matter to her. It's simple: he died, like all of us will. Just look outside and you'll see the same things: the murders, the unfairness, the predators, the prey, and the sun a silent witness to it all. To Liam, she is the embodiment of all things natural, of the world-as-is.

"How do you get out of bed in the morning, knowing what you know?" Liam asks as he fills her glass with wine.

"One leg at a time," Rebecca answers. "And grateful."

"Why?"

"Because I'm able. Because other people can't."

"What about Sparky? Doesn't what happened to him disturb

you? Scare you?"

"Sometimes. But I get over it."

"How?"

"By getting out of bed. One leg at a time. Grateful."

"Sounds easy."

"It is what it is."

Some guests begin to gather their children, coats, and dishes in preparation for departure, while Bob, Dick-Tracy, and some of the die-hards gather around the piano for Christmas carols. Liam and Rebecca continue to speak in the alcove off of the small sitting room. Their chairs bookend the fire as they face one another, their knees almost touching. A half-finished bottle of Bob's Cabernet rests on the floor between them. And just when the conversation steers toward Rebecca Kelly and the millions of things that have made her who she is, Little Napoleon rises again. He must know what this woman thinks of the stories. He needs praise.

"So," Liam stammers. "You read my stories, huh?"

Liam has often thought that his stories are simply broken bones and bruises on paper, a physical representation of all the things he's felt and seen in the last eighteen months. He wants someone to tell him his breaks will heal. Little Napoleon, on the other hand, wants her to tell him the breaks are beautiful.

"Yep," Rebecca answers. "I read 'em."

"Horrible, huh?"

"Liam, don't fish for compliments by insulting yourself. You know they're not horrible. What does it matter what I think anyway? I mean, that wasn't why you wrote them, was it?"

"No, I wrote 'em so I wouldn't hurt somebody."

"So what does it matter what I think?" she asks, taking a sip of wine.

"I don't know, to tell you the truth. It's just that you gave me that Whitman book and it reminded me of something...a way of looking at the world, of living. When I read that book the voice I heard was my brother's, like he was right beside me reading the lines. Like he and Walt were both pushing me somehow, encouraging me to go and face all those scary things outside. I felt like you were pushing me too. I guess I was just hoping my stories might push you somewhere as well." He stops, frightened he's exposed himself, frightened there might be no turning back. "I don't know what the hell I'm sayin', Rebecca, I just felt some kind of a connection between me and Sean and Walt and you. Does that sound crazy?"

"I've heard crazier," she says, poking the fire, sending sparks and burning embers up the chimney. "If it makes you feel any better, the stories did push me places. Places in the past I thought I'd forgotten, places my mind doesn't usually go."

Then she looks into the fire and begins to outline her impressions of the stories. Liam sits back, dumbfounded by her remarks.

She tells Liam she read the stories in two sittings, a bottle of cheap Rhine wine by her side. She listened to the Waterboys on her stereo and closed her eyes after reading the first story and thought about being a fisherman on the North Atlantic, anything to get away from dry land and its bitter memories. Then, after she read "Tiny Crosses," she watched the sunset and thought about the dusk, the time when the fleshy, the concrete, the delineated begins to blur into the nondescript. When the grass bleeds into itself and the growing shadows prevent you from seeing the individual blades, and you realize that, in the end, the differences between the blades of grass are both profound and hardly worth mentioning at all.

Then it struck her how the most banal things in the night–a cat, a street sign, an abandoned playground–can all take on ominous, significant, sometimes cosmic meaning if the observer is in a certain frame of mind. She tells Liam she remembered a distant uncle who was hit by a train on his sixteenth birthday and, although she never met him, she sometimes wonders what she might have missed.

Then she shakes her head and says, "Then, Liam, I started thinking about the damage this world does to us and all the things it gives us in return."

And as Liam sits listening, stunned, open-mouthed, she reaches over and puts her hand on his knee. It's like a jolt of electricity. She says, "Shit, Liam, none of that's important right now. The important thing is that the stories were written and you didn't have to hurt anyone. What matters is that we're here by this fire. On this night. In this house. C'mon, let's go sing Christmas carols with the others. It sounds like they could use our help. Bob's caterwauling is killing me."

* * *

Around the piano the last of the party gather. Dick and Tracy stand behind Linda as she plays, their arms wrapped around each other's shoulders. Glassy-eyed and joyous, they're happy that at last their search for home and companionship are through. The Madman and his date stand awkwardly in the doorway, unsure they wish to take part. Bob puts his arm around Rebecca and Liam as they approach, belting out a few words of "Come All Ye Faithful." Dick and Tracy smile and nod at the young couple, then bend down over Linda's shoulder to read the lyrics. At the conclusion of the song, more of the guests—including Hobart and Fink and the Madman—say their goodbyes and depart. Bob walks them to the door. After all the preparation and planning, the food and the drink and the laughter, the party is beginning to wind down. As the fella once said, all good things.

Returning from the foyer, Bob says, "Okay, Linda. Enough with the holiday fare. How about some dancing music? You know how the kids love to watch me dance. And I've got a little itch in my pants that can only be scratched with a little rock 'n roll."

Several children, ranging from four to fourteen years old, suddenly appear from the den where the inevitable "It's a Wonderful Life" plays on the television yet again. With shouts like, "Yeah, Mom, play 'Proud Mary'," and, "You gotta see this, my dad's like a bear when he dances," they gather at the walls to witness what they're sure will be another comic masterpiece of inept dance, courtesy of Big Bob Scallipari. Linda complies by playing "Brown-Eyed Girl."

At the carnivalesque beginning, Bob begins to gyrate across the parlor floor. Dick and Tracy, Rebecca and Liam and all the children begin to clap and laugh as Bob spins from one end of the room to the other. His shirt tails rise, exposing a large, hairy belly, and his beard glistens with sweat. Though Linda can't see her monstrous husband behind her, she sees his shadow at play on the wall before her and she too laughs because she can picture him clear as day. He keeps a straight face as he pirouettes and flails, prances and twirls. The children sing along. Then Dick and Tracy begin to dance as well, Tracy twirling Dick under his arm, shuffling loosely across the floor. Rebecca says to Liam as she grabs his hand, "C'mon, Liam, let's dance."

Content to watch the spectacle from afar, Liam refuses, saying, "I only dance after I've had about seventeen drinks or when I'm alone with Banshee in the guest house. You go ahead. I'll watch."

Despite his refusal, despite his fear that Little Napoleon will awake in the middle of the dance and make him self-consciously slink back to his seat, Rebecca simply won't take no for an answer. She pleads with him, holding his hand, and she's already dancing as Bob dips and dallies and sings about remembering when. And before Liam knows what's happening, he's moving to the center of the parlor and a beautiful redheaded woman is holding him in her arms, leading him around the makeshift dance floor. She leads and he follows.

So on this 23rd day of December in the parlor of a large Victorian house—with small children laughing and pointing, a large Italian named Bob making an ass of himself, and two flaming homosexuals frolicking and frisking—Liam and Rebecca dance for the very first time. And I could tell you that Liam smells apples in her hair and that her hands are slender yet her grip is strong. I could tell you his stomach flutters when—after a twirl—she pulls him to her, presses her breasts against him, and stares at him knowingly, like she's foreseen years of their future life together: the love-making, the children, the gardens, the wine. I could try to describe the liberation Liam feels at this moment, like chains and shackles are being loosed from his shoulders, body, and legs, making him feel like he can fly. Yeah, I could tell you all of that, but it would never approach the dance itself. Because these are just black words on a white page, not real life at all.

So if you wanna have some kind of idea what Liam's dance feels like, you're gonna have to put on a little Van Morrison, grab somebody who means something to you, and do some dancing of your own. It's the only way you'll understand something I've been trying to convince Liam of his whole life: that it's a hell of a lot better to dance than it is to read or write about somebody dancing. Because you can't live a life between the margins of a book You gotta stand up and do something, gotta be willing to forget the eyes of the spectators, the catcalls of the naysayers and pessimists, and say, "Fuck it. I'm going to dance while I'm still able."

C'mon, put the book down, throw some Van, Puffy, Merle, or B.B. on the stereo, and dance. It's better than you remember. And like I always tell Liam: dance now, you might not have another chance.

I bequeath myself to the dirt to grow from the grass I love,
If you want me again look for me under your bootsoles.
                                        –Walt Whitman

The Color of Grass
by
Liam McGarrity

As the May sun pounded down on us from above, the mourners gathered around the hole in which Sean would soon be laid to rest. We were uneasy, confused, waiting for the nightmare to end. Father Simpson spoke, squawking like Charlie Brown's teacher beside us.

"Waah, waah, waah-waah-waah."

It was hot, unusually muggy, and the men shuffled their feet and wiped the sweat from their brows then lifted their arms from their sides to air out their pits. The women—crumpled tissues in their hands—folded their arms and adjusted the sunglasses on their noses, the heat causing them to slip and fog and irritate. Wheeler stood at the curb waiting for the ceremony to conclude. The family sat in chairs right in front of the hole, staring dazedly before them. We looked spent, like we'd each been fighting that Opponent that my cousin Joseph had faced and had met a similar end. The Opponent had kicked our ass too.

"Brothers and waah-waahs," Father Simpson continued, periodically dabbing his forehead with a handkerchief. "Today we waah-waah, waah waah waah…"

The graves in Sean's vicinity were relatively new because the cemetery had only acquired the land a few years before. So the grass upon which the mourners, my family, and I were gathered was only recently planted and thus still fairly green, about the color of one of those limes they cut into eighths to put in Coronas. Only a year before Sean and I spent a lazy summer afternoon at a beach bar in Rosarito, Mexico–drinking Coronas with limes, talking to bikini-clad women and gum-peddling ninos, wondering how we could afford to live like this always. He was beautiful that day–smiling, laughing, dancing, speaking broken Spanish in such a way that even the most cynical waiter, even the most vitriolic hater of Americanos was enamored with him in the end. By sunset, a crowd of a dozen or so turistas and locals had gathered round our table, singing revolutionary songs, downing shots of tequila, dancing with stranger's wives, carrying stranger's children. I kissed a girl whose beer-chilled lips tasted of salt and lime and the sun. At the end of the night, each of the gathered assured one another that they would remain friends forever and abrazos were shared all around. Sean and I walked along the beach back to our campground.

But in contrast to the lime-colored grass at my feet were the rolls of beautiful new sod stacked in a pyramid directly behind the grave, just waiting to envelope my brother. That grass had long lush blades planted in thick loam, the soil dark, cool, brimming with the nutrients that would allow the blades to grow. The grass itself was verdant, plush, as green as kelp, much darker than the grass growing around me. How odd–I thought as I compared the new sod to the grass dying along the cemetery's edge–how odd to see the dead grass so near to the new, the dying things so close to the strong.

"Waah, waah, waah-waah-waah."

I looked up the hill to my left, in the direction of Mom's grave, to include her in the ceremony. The grass up there was all the same color, mostly dead or dying, white with scalped roots, littered with briars and burrs and connected with the sideways growth of the crabgrass. So fitting, I thought, that the crabgrass enveloped Mom's final home. Crabgrass. The crab. Cancer, the sign of the crab. Even in death the crab was getting her, even in death cancer would not let her go. Around her grave, the soil was hard, almost gray, cracking from the heat, the crust of the earth damn near impossible to penetrate. Nobody complained about the condition of the grass or the soil near those graves, though, because they were old and as the years passed fewer and fewer visitors paid them any mind.

They didn't care that (by order of the diocese) the older graves were watered less to conserve money. The survivors had grown accustomed to the hard soil and cancerous grass because they'd grown hard too. They'd grown familiar with their loss, their hearts as closed as the crusty layer of soil atop the holes that had been so fresh and prominent only twenty or thirty years before.

In contrast to Mom's grave, there were rectangular patches of lush, avocado-green grass sprinkled throughout the cemetery, covering those that had died in the past weeks. It seemed to me that the people who visited the older graves forgot that on the new graves the grass is green and cool to the touch and if you walk on it barefoot it tickles your feet. The soil beneath the fresh sod is filled with worms and roly-poly bugs, easy to penetrate with a finger or a shovel should you decide to plant flowers. The contrast between the white grass of the older graves and the green grass of the newer ones was stark and as I looked at the fresh green patches littered throughout the cemetery, I knew they covered fresh holes in the earth, represented fresh wounds in someone else's life.

Then the months pass–the rains, the sun, the other deaths–and the new grass begins to blend in with the color of the grass beside it. It no longer receives the extra water; it no longer stands in stark contrast to the older graves. Eventually all the deaths run together like those around my mom's. It's only a matter of time until the new graves become old and the grass that was once so long, green, and cool grows blanched and turns the color of the grass by my mom's grave. Then the crabgrass connects the dying grass and you can't tell where one grave ends and another one begins. The individual holes are united and the separate deaths blend into a general sense of malaise.

That is to say, it's only a matter of time until the color of the grass allows us to forget the individual dead.

"Waah-waah, you might ask," Father Simpson continued. "After all, waah-waah is not a waah-waah anymore, true?"

On the outskirts of the proceedings, two Mexican cemetery workers stood leaning on shovels. One was probably about nineteen years old and wore knee-high rubber waders stained with mud. He looked bored, a little exasperated he had to stand in the sun until the service was over. Although young, he'd obviously become inured to the ritual at play before him. The other man was about forty years old and his leathered, crevassed face evidenced his lifetime of work in the sun. He wore faded jeans and the knee of the right leg was holey from when he'd bent down to adjust the cemetery sprinklers. A plaid flannel shirt unbuttoned halfway down his torso revealed a gold crucifix that hung on his chest, glistening periodically when the sun hit it at just the right angle. He held a Los Angeles Dodgers baseball cap–curved bill, sweat-stained–in his left hand, the shovel in his right. He leaned forward to hear Father Simpson, like the priest whispered secrets only he could decipher.

"Ashes to ashes. Dust to dust. Waah-waah to waah-waah, in the name of the waah-waah, the waah-waah, and the holy waah-waah."

I found out later that the older Mexican hailed from Guadalajara, Mexico, and lived with about fifteen other illegals in a rented house in Santa Ana. They came across the border somewhere in Arizona, driving a truck with a faulty water pump that had been pieced together in Juarez by an uncle who had acquired parts from half a dozen stolen Fords. That was twenty years before and in all that time the man had learned about a hundred words of English. So even if he heard Father Simpson's speech, he couldn't understand its meaning. Though he didn't know what the hell the priest was talking about, his wrinkled forehead and forward-leaning torso displayed the machinations of a man trying to ascertain some truth. His name was Javier.

Opposite the two workers, below the cemetery, was a long shallow canyon that looked like a mirage. It stretched about three miles across, but its length was indiscernible because the ends of it disappeared into the hazy suffusion of the oddly interminable May heat. The air trembled above the canyon and the trees hovered within it like their roots were not in the ground, like they were waiting to be sucked into the sky by the suspiration of some mighty being. Yellow brush colored the embankment on the far side and the scene was so still it looked like a painting. But then in the distance I saw a rider on a black horse trotting along a faded path that ran the canyon's length. I imagined the rider to be some emissary of Death, a courier trying to find a way to relate some arcane and antique message to one person among thousands who might understand. The rider verified that the scene of which I was a part was no painting or mirage, it was the accretion of some of the most concrete and verifiable things there are: broken bodies, widows, orphans.

While the chatter of the priest continued, I looked out on that dreamy canyon as if the past might be contained there, lost amid the trembling waves of heat, perhaps trampled beneath the hooves of that mysterious rider. I then thought of my history there at St. Brendan's Cemetery: the small Christmas trees we put on Mom's grave, the Lakers' games Sean and I listened to on the radio with her there beneath us, the Mother's Day's flowers we brought her every year; then the driving lessons, the beers, the meditation, the discussions with the dead, the way the cemetery grew and grew and grew. I felt at home in St. Brendan Cemetery because I'd been there so many times before. All the other funeral-goers must have thought I was a little crazy, because–as Father Simpson waah-waahed his way through the wooden conclusion of his rehearsed monologue–I laughed out loud, thinking that bedrooms, bars, books, and graveyards are some of the only places where I feel completely at home.

But now I realize that isn't funny at all. It's really just kind of pathetic.

* * *

The first time I went to St. Brendan Cemetery was when we had to pick out a plot for my mom the day after she died. (I always hated that word "plot." Like the place you bury people has anything to do with the unfolding of a story, the parts of a narrative. The only part of a story that exists in cemetery plots is the part after the last period, the part that says "The End.") My dad wanted me to stay at home with my Aunt Maureen because he thought it would be too traumatic for me, but I insisted on going with him, wherever he went. For about a month after Mom died, I clung to his leg because I'd already lost one parent and I sure as hell didn't want to lose two. I figured if somebody took him somewhere they'd have to take me with them. There was no way in hell I was letting go of that skinny leg of his.

The uneasy, poorly shaved man working in St. Brendan's office showed us a blueprint of the cemetery and which of the numbered plots were available to purchase. The plans were blue like the plans of houses my dad always spread on our kitchen counter after work, the ones where the kitchens and living rooms were always much bigger than ours. It struck me that buying a plot for a grave was a lot like buying a plot for a condominium or a dream house, because you want the one with the best view but it always costs ya just a little bit more. The man tried to convince my dad to buy a family plot with room enough for the six of us because cemetery plots—like donuts—are cheaper by the half dozen. But my dad told him no, he couldn't afford it. Besides, the next plot he'd need to buy would be his own, he thought, and somebody else would have to foot the bill for that one.

A lot of people want money so that they can buy that new Mercedes, that house in Newport, the ephemera of this fading world. But not me. I think the only good reason to be rich is to be able to buy as many cemetery plots as you need to house your whole family together after they die. That's the only purchase that has any real staying power, any lasting value. Even Veblin would have to admit that there's no planned obsolescence in the grave business. Hell, if I had money I'd buy a whole cemetery just so that my family and friends could be together at the end. I'd make my own rules, run it the right way, because the cemeteries in California are so vanilla and non-descript. The tributes they pay are so weak and pathetic. At St. Brendan's, the headstones lay flat in the ground so you can't find a grave until you're standing over the top of it. There are no large crypts, no trumpeting angels in marble, no sense that we yearn to understand the unexplainable.

But my cemetery would be different. I'd wire the place with an elaborate stereo system, hide those tiny Bose speakers all over the place, and each mourner could spin their own tunes. There'd be a central library of musical selections from which to choose. One day you could listen to Mozart's Requiem, the next day you could listen to Jackson Browne. I'd have a regular library too. You could read Rilke's *Duino Elegies* one morning and the poems of Cavafy the next. I'd install barbeques and picnic benches; maybe dot the landscape with chilled kegs of Budweiser and Murphy's. Polite

Irish bartenders would pour you drinks and listen to you laugh and cry as you tried to connect with the departed the only way you know how: in stories, memories, and dreams. I'd hire a mason to build paths between the graves and tell him to imbed stones and twigs and mementos in his handiwork so the living realize that—like the tokens in the masonry—one day they too will be frozen forever in time. I'd water the grass twice, maybe three times a day, so that it stayed greener and more alive, so that we could never forget the dead. Headstones thirty feet high would adorn the graves, decorated with scenes from the life that has passed, decked with joyful hopes for some kind of life in the future.

Yeah, I'd like to be rich so that I could run a cemetery the right way, so that my mom's and brother's graves weren't so far away from each other. Because when you're poor your dead are scattered all over the place.

My mom died in August and the following May, on Mother's Day, I played the subtraction game for the first time. The whole family walked down the hill to the jacaranda beside her grave. As Sean cleaned the headstone with a wet rag, I looked out at the lake (the canyon was filled with water at that time) then at Mom's headstone, thinking of the papers my Aunt Rose showed me when she came from Buffalo for the funeral. The papers contained stories, poems, and songs that my mother had written during her sickness. Hundreds of pages of notes, ideas, ballads. It was in those papers that I discovered that my mom wanted to live in a house above a lake. In her scribbled handwriting she described the house and she must have known that she was dying and she'd never have any new houses, never live beside any lakes, but she continued to write, to describe things that would only exist in her mind.

And as I stood beside her grave on that first Mother's Day I saw Mom's handwriting on those pages again—the big loops on her handwritten B's, the tiny a's that were sometimes beside them—and I realized that I'd never see her write again, never see *her* again, and I felt the tears rising within me. I fought them because I didn't want to cry and my dad to think I was a mama's boy. So, to distract myself from the fact that Mom was dead, I started to study the headstones of the graves around hers. Some had pictures of Jesus on them; some had the Virgin Mary, some simple crosses. Then I looked at the years on the stones and subtracted the smaller numbers from the larger ones to see how old the people were when they died. The grave next to Mom's read:

> Mildred A. Becker
> 1928-1974
> Beloved Wife and Mother
> May She Rest in Peace

Seventy-four minus twenty-eight, fourteen minus eight is six, less one, six minus two is four . . . Forty-six. Mildred was forty-six when she died, I thought.

But the subtraction backfired because my mom was forty-six when she died, too. That didn't help me forget. So I moved on to the next gravestone and subtracted again. 1946-1949. Forty-nine minus forty-six. Wow, that kid was only three, just a baby. Next. 1903-1945. Forty-two; must have been a war guy; it says he was a captain. 1879-1963. A little different. Gotta add twenty-one to sixty-three. Holy shit, eighty-four years old, two lifetimes really. I'd move on down the line, subtracting the numbers, preoccupying myself with the information on the gravestones, instead of focusing on what lay beneath them.

Over the years Sean took me to visit my mom periodically, mostly when we should have been at church. When I asked him why we didn't go to church anymore, he looked down at Mom's grave and said we *were* at church. Sean taught me to drive at St. Brendan's when I was only fourteen. I asked him why he only let me drive inside the gates of the cemetery and he said, "You can't hurt anybody here. These people are about as hurt as you can get, bro."

After I got my license (Sean's lessons worked) I could go to the cemetery by myself, escape the noises that sometimes arise in a motherless household: the screaming, the loud televisions, the drunken questions asked of nobody in particular. It was comforting to lay beside my mom's grave and look to the sky and realize that she was in the same position as me only six feet away. It was like she was behind me, pushing me toward the sun.

That was when I started talking to the dead. I'd talk to her about all the things that occupied my adolescent mind–Mr. Wilt's English class, Coach Macklin and our horrible football team, *The Shining* and The Overlook Hotel–and I did it openly because I figured since she was dead she probably knew everything there was to know about me anyway. She'd already seen what I did to myself in the shower and what I did to my girlfriend on the weekend, so there was no need to lie to her like my friends did to their moms. Besides, dead mothers are easier to talk to because they don't judge or condemn, they don't yell at you when you're late or criticize your girlfriends when they disapprove of them. Dead mothers encourage you to get things off your chest. In fact, now that I think about it, dead mothers are better than living ones because they never interrupt you when you're talking. The only problem with dead mothers is that they're unable to offer advice when it's needed most. But I guess you can't have everything.

After our conversations I listened to the wind as it flitted through the jacaranda and pushed the clouds across the sky. The sparrows sang and the ducks swam in the lake below. I dozed there on the grass and the jets from the El Toro Marine Base sometimes ripped the silence, but even they seemed small and powerless against the largeness of it all. Occasionally a tractor rumbled past–its diesel exhaust going to the sky like dissipating black blades of grass –as it went to dig another grave. But mostly it was just me and my mom and the quiet. Peace.

You know, the quiet of cemeteries is the deepest quiet there is because there are more people saying nothing. Cemeteries are history incarnate because all the hushed lives are there. They're pregnant with the silence of the dead and, for that reason, so much more alive.

* * *

But as I sat beside the grave in which Sean was to be buried and the ceremony proceeded around me (waah-waah, waah-waah, waah), I realized that the quiet had left the cemetery again. I was starting over. Once again we were picking out a burial plot and casket, once again we were faced with a year filled with firsts: the first Christmas, the first Laker game, Easter, Thanksgiving, etc.

And every step between my mom's and Sean's grave was like a step down that mythical ladder of prosperity, a reminder that my dad didn't have enough money to purchase enough gravestones for us all. Chaos and noise once again gained the upper hand and I couldn't make sense of any of it. There was no justification for what had happened.

Since I could see no reason for Sean's death, no reason that hole before me needed to be dug, I figured I'd wait for it to appear. If one existed, I thought it would be near his grave, in the air or the trees or the grass. So for about a month after he died I went to his grave every day to listen, to watch, to try and see something, anything, that might make his death sensible or justified.

That was when I started to notice Javier and the difference between the grasses. I went to Sean's grave the day after the funeral to watch them plant the grass. Javier was the crew chief. He drove the tractor they used to fill the hole that was now filled with my brother, while the others leaned on shovels around it. In a cloud of dust, with the tractor creaking and rumbling, they covered the casket then leveled the soil with their shovels. The other workers unrolled the sod carefully, making sure it did not tear, while Javier carefully observed from his perch on the tractor. The new sod was pristine and moist. No weeds, brown spots, or pests on it. Just the beautiful uncut hair of graves, like Walt called it. The men worked hurriedly because the sod must be planted and watered quickly if it hopes to survive the brutal onslaught of the California sun. The sod contrasted with the older grass near Sean's grave, which was browning in the spots where a broken sprinkler couldn't reach it. I looked all over the cemetery and saw the rookie mourners sitting beside their dark green symbols of loss, the flowers beside them wilting in the sun.

I visited Sean's fresh hole every day and after about a week I started to realize how much things had changed there since my mom died. There were three tractors instead of one and they'd purchased some land across Crookhaven Road so there were more graves to be dug, more work to be done. The parking lot behind the office had been expanded and there were at least five cars parked in it at any one time. More workers milled in and out of the large steel shed on the cemetery's perimeter, more dead spilled out of more hearses as they filled the earth with more corpses, more seeds for more potential lives.

More noise.

A clamor ruled St. Brendan's, a din that wasn't there when Mom died. Business there was steady and everyone knows that, no matter the industry, good business leaves a tumult in its wake. It seemed like I wouldn't be at Sean's grave for ten minutes before a dump truck's beeping would notify me it was headed in reverse, an earthmover would rumble and metallically shake, or a tractor's diesel engine would destroy my silence. More often than not the man on the tractor was Javier, going from one fresh grave to another, digging and riding and kissing his crucifix every time he passed one of those rectangular patches of new sod. He took his hands from the steering wheel and crossed himself afterwards and bobbed up and down on his tractor while riding over the bumps in the dirt below the cemetery, like a pious jack-in-the-box on wheels.

We were both at the cemetery doing our work and it was a matter of about a week before Javier noticed me there every day, watching him do his job. One evening, a little after five o'clock, I pulled through the gates of the cemetery and Javier was walking out of the offices. I instinctively waved to him and he nodded in response. >From that moment it was like Javier was a hovering bird of prey who flew in circles around me and the circles got smaller and smaller until the day—about three weeks after the burial—I was studying Sean's new headstone. I was looking at the dates (August 7, 1970-May 16, 2000) doing my usual subtraction thing (thinking about how close Sean made it to his thirtieth birthday, wondering if I'd ever make it to my mine) when I felt a human presence beside me. Javier was standing there with knee-high boots and a plastic six-pack holder with four Budweisers still in it. He held it at his hip like it was a gun in a holster. His gold crucifix shone in the late afternoon sun and his chest stuck out like he wanted everyone to know he wore it. He handed me a can and I knew the distance that separated us was greater than the two feet between us.

"Cerveza?" he asked.

I reached for the beer and back into my mind for what Spanish I knew and said, "Si. Gracias."

He pointed to the grave and asked, "Quien es?"

"Mi hermano," I answered.

When he heard my answer he looked to the dry bed beneath the cemetery and squinted his black eyes in the sun. From the wrinkles around his eyes I could tell that squinting was a habit of his, like he looked into the sun a lot.

He pointed at his chest and said, "Javier," I did the same and said, "Liam."

We drank the beers in silence. Javier wiped his forehead with the arm that held his sweat-stained Dodgers cap. Then he looked at the gravestone and raised two fingers to me like he was Churchill. "Huh? Huh?" he asked, his eyes growing large, hoping I could understand. I didn't know what he was trying to tell me so I looked at him, shrugged, and asked, "Que?" Then he set his beer on the ground, held up nine fingers with his two hands and it dawned on me that he too subtracted the numbers on gravestones to calculate the age of the deceased.

Excitedly I said, "Si, twenty . . . ahhh veinte . . . nueve. Tenia veintinueve anos. Es todo."

Javier looked into the distance again and laughed as he thought something to himself. Then he looked at me and held his middle finger to the sky, flipping off the sun or maybe some god or beast in which he believed. Looking at the gold crucifix on his chest, I wondered what the hell his religion was.

"Fuck Heem, huh?" he screamed, pointing his finger toward the sky. "Fuck Heem!"

I laughed and nodded and looked into the top of my beer and said, "Si, Javier. Fuck Him."

After we'd finished a beer apiece and were feeling their liberating effects, Javier signaled for me to hop on his tractor. I held my fresh beer in one hand and his shoulder in the other and stood behind him as we rumbled to the other side of St. Brendan's. The grass on that side of the cemetery was all the same color and you couldn't tell where one grave's grass began and the one beside it ended. But the grass directly below where we stopped was a strangely beautiful green, like it'd somehow gotten more water than the other older graves. We parked at the curb and walked down the incline. Javier stopped and pointed to a gravestone that read:

Enrique Fernandez
1980-1994
Querido Hijo y Hermano

(Ninety-four minus eighty equals fourteen.) Javier pointed to the marker dejectedly and said, "Es *mi* hermano." I bowed my head, said "Claro, claro," then reached both my middle fingers to the sky so Javier would know I understood.

Fuck Him.

After that day I went to the cemetery in the late afternoon so that Javier and I could share a few beers after our work was through. Javier tried to teach me some more Spanish and I tried to teach him a few more words of English, but, like always, the most essential things were lost in translation. I wanted to know why the grass around his brother's grave was still green. He knew what I was asking, I think, but he only shrugged his shoulders and laughed, refusing to admit he understood my query. We gave up on the language lessons after a time because it ruined the silence both of us enjoyed. Sitting quietly drinking our beers, we conceived thoughts in our respective languages and threw them to the dead in our own particular way. The sun, the beers, and the dead brothers were the only language Javier and I had, but stronger than any words I'd ever known.

And slowly, St. Brendan's began to get peaceful again. I just needed to go at the right time, after work when the tractors and other heavy machinery had stopped, after hours, when the other people had gone.

Sean's death was like the new pair of pointed cowboy boots I bought to wear at his funeral. They pinched my feet when I first tried them on. They hurt. Then time passed and I wore them some more: at my uncle's funeral, at O'Malley's wedding, on a couple of dates. And they became more comfortable, softer on my heel and looser around my toes. Then before I knew it they weren't new boots anymore, they were part of my wardrobe, molded to my body. I got used to my new boots and to the fact that my brother was dead. It takes a lot of time to become comfortable with painful things, but it happens, and in time the pain actually mellows and softens, like worn leather. Don't ask me how, but, like an old pair of worn cowboy boots, your loss becomes comforting in the end.

* * *

The last time I went to St. Brendan's before I returned to my life in Colorado was several months after Sean died. The morning grass was wet with the dew and the nine o'clock sun came gently through the sky like a shy child sneaking into his parents' morning bed–slowly, like it didn't want to be noticed. I brought a bucket of water and an old white T-shirt so that I could polish Sean's headstone one last time. Little pieces of cut grass clung to my socks, refusing to go away after the mower's blades had killed them, refusing to die at all. I walked down the hill toward the grave and nodded in my mom's direction to let her know I'd see her after I visited Sean.

Nothing could have surprised me more than what I saw at Sean's grave. It looked like a party. Deirdre and Erin and Brigid were sitting on a blanket eating bagels. My sister Molly held Nora's new baby and Nora watched her other daughter teeter as she walked. I went to them, amazed.

"What the hell are you guys doing here?" I asked.

Molly said, "Good to see you too," and told me that it'd been six months that day since Sean died. I shook my head because I couldn't believe it'd been that long, because even now it doesn't seem like a year-and-a-half that he's been dead, but it is.

I kissed everyone and sat down on the blanket. There were wet tissues, opened cream cheese containers, cartons of orange juice, and plastic knives littered across it. The adults sat in a broken circle, watching the children laugh and play and do somersaults down the hill. It was only when Nora's oldest walked to the edge of the blanket and over the top of Sean's grave, that I noticed you couldn't tell the difference between the color of Sean's grass and that of the grass around it. The patch had disappeared. The lime-colored grass of the previous years and the plush green of the fresh sod, had bled into one another and become some hybrid mix, some separate breed of grass never found before. The blades of the new creation entwined and swallowed the hole that was so obvious only months before. And I thought, wow, time changed the color of the grass.

But something was strange, different about the color of the grass around Sean's grave. It was as if his grave was the center of a circle and in a radius of about twenty yards the grass was as green as a freshly picked avocado. It was a bit longer than the grass beyond it and much more vibrant and alive. There was no crabgrass or dandelions, no defects of neglect. The grass in that circle was just long enough for the wind to blow it, for the departing dead to make it move. It occurred to me that Javier must have set the timers for the sprinklers so that Sean's grave would get more water than the other graves, just like he did to his own brother's.

"I'll be damned," I muttered, shaking my head in disbelief. "That Mexican son of a bitch."

It's funny, I wanted the grass to stay green because then I would never become hardened to Sean's death, would never act like it was completely in the past. But if it was too green–like the day of the funeral–it would be overwhelming and the hole beneath it would be too apparent, making it impossible to live my own life at all. There's got to be a certain shade of green I've not yet seen on any grave, that might allow you to live your life fully, but still not forget the dead. There's got to be a certain green hue that cuts through the differences between life and death. I think Javier and I are both trying to find that perfect color green, the one that will remind, but not paralyze us. So we search and plant and water, dig and study and watch. We experiment with different types of manure, mow at odd intervals, try the best we can, but we're only men, and, like so many men before us, our means of reckoning and measurement are so very feeble and flawed.

Deirdre said, "Let's tell stories about him. That's when I'm happiest."

So we did. I told them a story about brothers who ask each other questions in the night and the rebels they try to emulate. I told them about Little Napoleon, tiny crosses, and priests who drink whiskey. Molly talked about the first day she beat Sean in basketball and how he threw the ball about a hundred feet in the air, but later was proud to tell everyone his sister had earned a basketball scholarship to UCLA. Nora told us how she talks to Sean and sometimes feels warmth on her knee, like he's there comforting her somehow. Deirdre wanted to talk about their trailer by the lake, the quiet nights with the kids, the bedroom they shared, but the words got stuck in her throat.

We told stories around his grave like it was a campfire, like the words mixed with the grass was the only source of heat in the world, and though the warmth was slight it was certainly better than no heat at all.

After an hour or so, Margaret and Catherine Hurley, two long-time friends of the family, showed up with a bouquet of flowers about three feet wide. Margaret laughed and showed me the ribbon across the front of the flowers that read, "Today's Your Birthday. Congratulations!"

"It was the only bouquet left in the shop," Margaret said. "Some debutante's mother bought the rest for her damn daughter's afternoon party."

She set the flowers on the grave and pulled out a six-pack of Miller Genuine Draft from her backpack. She poured a beer for Sean, the grass atop his grave thirstily absorbing it, like Sean himself drank those Coronas one year before. Deirdre pointed to a sign that was erected about fifty feet away that read, "NO ALCOHOL ON CEMETERY PROPERTY." Amazingly, it was the only sign of its kind in the whole cemetery and stood in the corner beside Sean's grave. It'd been put up sometime in the last six months. I walked to the sign, pulled it from the dirt, and hurled it into the shrubs below the cemetery's property, trying to throw it in the canyon below. Erin asked me why I threw the sign and I told her what my brother, her father, had told me all those years before:

"Erin, never let a piece of metal tell you what you should or should not do."

Deirdre said, "Nice example, Uncle Liam, destroying private property."

"I had a great teacher," I replied.

On my way back up the hill, I noticed my dad's red Toyota truck parked on Crookhaven at the curb above the grave. A blue line of smoke wafted upward to the ever-boldening sky. His left arm was out the window and he was probably listening to a talk radio program on some topic he couldn't give a shit about. I knew that he'd never come down to the grave with the rest of us; he'd never let any of us know he missed his wife and son.

Then, like an army of militant gophers mounting a sneak attack, the automatic sprinklers popped from the ground all around us and we had no time to react. We were sopped in an instant. It was that bastard Javier's extra water coming for the grass.

Chook-chook, chook-chook, chook-chook, the sprinklers hummed.

The girls screamed and my sisters grabbed the babies and Catherine and Margaret grabbed the beers. Deirdre held her girls' hands and I snatched the blanket and began to run up the hill after the others. I slipped on the wet incline and put my hand down to catch myself.

Chook-chook, chook-chook, chook-chook.

I'm not sure what it was, whether it was the looseness from my beer, the lightness I felt from telling all the stories, or the fact that it looked like the sun was shedding the moisture from itself, like the white drops and the heat were both spraying from the sun's wheel. I don't know what it was, but something made me stop my retreat. I dropped the blanket on the wet grass and looked at the beckoning sun above me. I rubbed the water on my arms and ran my fingers through my black hair.

Chook-chook, chook-chook, chook-chook.

Slowly, I walked back to Sean's grave. Atop the grass I began to spin in a slow circle, gaining speed as I went, my head thrown back and arms spread wide. With eyes closed, I felt the heat and the water attack my pale skin. I spun and laughed and heard someone scream. When I opened my eyes I saw Erin and Brigid sliding down the grassy hill on their stomachs, playing with me in the water and the sun. The rest of the entourage followed our lead and returned to the graveside. We squealed and laughed, we yelled and skipped. Then we ran around Sean's grave in a circle, our hands entwined, shouting a meaningless chant like we were dancing gypsies at a wedding. "Hey, hey, hey, hey!"

Chook-chook, chook-chook, chook-chook.

I looked up to the curb and saw my dad laughing outside his truck with a cigarette still in his hand. Then I looked in the direction of my mom's grave to include her in the celebration.

Chook-chook. Hey, hey. Chook-chook. Hey, hey.

And there he was, Javier the Mexican landscaper, standing just outside the radius of his sprinklers, blue Dodgers cap in hand. He stood in almost the exact same spot as six months before, when he so futilely tried to understand the words of the priest whose time had gone. There was no trouble with the communications this time, though. He watched the water arc away from its source and drop gently to the ground. Falling soft and light, light and soft, the grass silently absorbing it like a thirsty child. He felt the sun on his chest and knew what all the elements—including the imprint of our feet—were doing to the color of the grass. Maybe that's the one thing most needed to make the grass on graves the right color: the imprint of dancing feet.

Javier stared at all of us as we danced and clapped his hands in time. He mouthed our words as we screamed them and seemed to understand everything. He was laughing his ass off.

Chook-chook. Hey, hey.

Chook-chook.

Hey, hey.

The Light

SEVEN

My dad would sooner cut off an arm than let a neighbor know he needs a cup of sugar. The man is old school Irish. You don't talk about your family's problems; never admit you have a weakness or a need. So if he knew all the things Liam has written about our family, he'd shit. I haven't helped matters much, I guess, the way I've been running off at the mouth, but the cat's out of the bag and there's nothing to be done about it now. You already know the McGarrity's cling desperately to the past, are as inflexible as steel rods, have raging tempers, believe dead people cause the wind, despise the rich, have a fondness for the drink, are haunted by the sun, and eat like famished plow horses.

At this point it couldn't hurt to tell you that Liam's not the only member of the family to hear voices. We all do. Every single one of us. Hold on, hold on, I'm not talking about Jeffrey Dahmer, kill-the-mailman-and-eat-his-biceps, kind of voices; I'm talking about other kinds. You know, like in *Animal House* when that girl passes out at the party and the guy has an angel on one shoulder telling him to do certain things and a devil on the other telling him to do other things. I don't know if it's the norm, but the McGarrity's hear people–both dead and alive–like they set up shop in our friggin' heads. But, hey, what are you gonna do? You can't choose whose blood is running through your veins.

When I was alive, I used to put my voices into two categories. It made things simpler. In one category were the voices that told me to be careful, do what's best for myself, stay alive at any cost.

People like Richard Nixon, Tom Clancy, and other tight-ass reactionaries fell into this category. But I tried to listen to the voices in the second category, the voices that told me to give away what I have, forget about myself, and take a chance whenever the opportunity arises. People like Brendan Behan, Muhammad Ali, and my mom fell into this category. Hell, I even listened to folks who never actually lived. People like Lucas Jackson and R. P. McMurphy. I know it ain't much, but this poor man's philosophy always served me well. I jumped from airplanes, climbed steep mountains, rode unsaddled horses, fathered two beautiful children, all because I refused to play it safe, refused to cling and grasp. Yeah, I have no regrets about the short life I led.

If Liam classified his voices like I did, he'd have Little Napoleon in the anal-retentive column and Walt, Rebecca, and me in the other. For the past eighteen months the rest of us have had a hard time getting through to the kid because of the belligerent ravings of that French lunatic. He would tell Liam to rewrite a certain paragraph a dozen times, anything to preserve himself forever in print, anything to avoid risking death and all the impenetrable mysteries in the sun.

"Mon frere, zees ees pathetique, non? How weel we get published eef you refuse to listen to moi? Maintenant, zees ees what we'll do…"

Liam listened to that frog while the sun rose and set, day after day, month after month, the drama unfolding while Liam refused his part. His life was passing him by.

Now, Liam sits at his table with a warm cup of tea in his hand, trying to sort out his voices. He rose at 4:44 when Banshee whined to go outside and he's been up since. He read some *Leaves*, washed the wine glasses from last night, put a fire in the fireplace, and made a pot of Barry's. As he dried the dishes at the sink, Liam looked over his shoulder at Rebecca asleep on his futon. He smiled. Ah, a little peace, love, and understanding, Liam thought as he looked at Rebecca. The first time in a long time. But that sense of peace left Liam moments ago. As he folded his dishtowel and crept past the table (trying not to awaken Rebecca) on his way to retrieve the paper, Liam heard Little Napoleon's voice yet again. Where, he wondered, where is the little bastard now? Why can't I shut him out completely? I thought he died last night when Rebecca and I were dancing.

"Liam," the frog whispered. *"You've had your leetle fun. Maintenant, get her out of here. Tout de suite. We have more work to do. Ze revision of ze last story is more important zan any of zese, zese, zese shenanigans. Vite, vite!"*

Liam stopped abruptly and sat at the table, momentarily at a loss. I thought that little bastard was dead, he thought. Where can he be now? Then, after staring a few minutes at the stack of stories on the table–the stories he's been hiding in a guest house, bar, and market, writing–a smile slowly came to Liam's lips. He had a revelation, realized what a fool he had been. Yeah, Liam finally realized that Little Napoleon didn't die with me in May like he'd imagined. He'd just gone underground while his wounds were healing, adopted a more devious approach to secure his ends. Instead of leading Liam to obvious conquests in the classroom, football field, and bedroom, for the past eighteen months Little Napoleon has been concealed in every line of Liam's writing, nestled between commas, huddled behind m's and s's and y's. His injured little man realized he couldn't defeat the sun with his belligerence, couldn't live forever in the face of its power, so he tried to secure his immortality another way: through the publication of a book of short stories. Little Napoleon would live forever in Liam's prose, the star of a book he convinced Liam to write.

"The subterfuging son of a bitch," Liam mutters aloud.

Now, as he stares at the stories with hands folded, Liam hears the struggling, pugnacious part of himself–the one that fights Death, questions the cosmos, and wants to live forever–screaming at him from every page. And he understands that he's been ignoring the most noble parts of himself, the parts that risk and yearn and reach and climb and allow everything to go when the time requires. He's been listening to the wrong voices all along. Yeah, it took the thickheaded kid awhile, but now he understands what I've been telling you guys for a while now: that writing can sometimes be a feeble excuse not to live.

So he reaches across the table and picks up the stack of stories. He flips the pages against his cheek, smelling the ink and the paper, feeling the coolness of their lifeless weight. Then he thumbs through the stories slowly, stopping occasionally to read a random passage, selecting sentences in the middle of long paragraphs, smiling at epigrams from Walt throughout. And for the first time, the stories are something separate from him, something apart from his blood and pain, his memory and muscle. They are no longer bruises on paper, no longer blood-ink strewn across an uncaring palette. No, they are simply words that have helped him accept what had been so unacceptable just eighteen months ago. Liam sees now that the stories are just a bridge that allows him to cross to the next part of his life. The part where *I'm* the brother who's dead and he's the brother that's alive.

Little Napoleon be damned, he thinks, I can't listen to him anymore.

So he rises from the chair and walks to the fireplace at the foot of the futon where Rebecca and Banshee sleep. He sits on the ground before the fire, his stories held loosely in his right hand. For a few moments, he holds the paper and looks over his shoulder at Rebecca–silently measuring her breaths, thinking of the heart beating in her chest, curious about the dreams churning in her mind. Her red hair is splayed like a red paint bomb against the white pillow and her hands are raised above her head like she's surrendering in an old western. Banshee is nestled close to her body, her eyes fighting to stay open. Then Liam looks at the stack of paper in his hand and the fire beside him. Rebecca breathes and lives, the paper doesn't breathe at all. He has to make a choice.

Again I don't wanna go Swayze on you, but at this instant I am here with him, encouraging him to do what he must, no matter the fear, no matter the uncertainty.

But Little Napoleon rises one last time, saying, *"Mais non, Liam, what are you theenking? Huh? After all our time together, all ze beautiful words and stories we composed, how could you even theenk eet? Pull yourself together, mon frere, we've got much work to do..."*

Liam whispers, "You ain't my fuckin' brother, so stop calling me that. And I've listened to you long enough."

I say, "Let it go, Liam. Sure, there's a lot of things you can't control out there under the sun–the death, the cancer, the bad golf shots–but so is everything worth living for. C'mon, bro, do it. This is all you have for now."

And, like he hears me loud and clear, Liam takes the stack of paper, the first page of which reads, "The Death of Little Napoleon," and throws it on the fire. The flame in the fireplace is momentarily stifled beneath the weight of the tome, but slowly the corners of the pages turn orange then brown then black. The blue flames lick the edges then slowly consume the rest and the wispy smoke rises up the chimney and disappears into the predawn Colorado sky. The pages crinkle and smolder and burn and, in just a few moments time, they are gone. "So easy," Liam thinks, "so simple to do. I just had to listen to Sean again, try and do what he would do." He lets the flames dance across his face and he puts his hands to the fire and laughs because—like last night when he danced—the sense of release is visceral in his stomach. And though he's a large man with big shoulders, at this moment Liam feels like a waif, like he could fly away if given the chance.

Then he feels a hand on the back of his neck. He does not turn to her, he simply puts his chin to his chest and lets Rebecca caress him. Her fingers are warm, her hair tickles his ear lightly, and he's never been happier in his life.

And for the first time since I was alive, the kid's listening to the voices he should. It just goes to show you that—no matter what those candy-ass shrinks say—hearing voices in your head ain't such a bad thing, it's only when you listen to the *wrong* voices, the Jeffrey-Dahmer type, that you get yourself in trouble.

* * *

It is half past six on a twenty-eight degree, Christmas Eve morning. The predawn sky is frigid and filled with a fading gibbous moon. Liam and Rebecca walk out the door of the guesthouse, Banshee on a leash before them. Rebecca wears a black stocking cap pulled low over her forehead, a heavy wool coat, and thick gloves, yet the chill Colorado air still makes her shiver. She wraps her arms through Liam's elbow and buries her face against his chest, trying to warm her flushed cheeks. Liam momentarily rests his chin atop her head, then lurches forward as Banshee pulls him along.

185

Out the side gate, through the intersection of Hyperion and Grian, they walk toward the Denver Freedom Park—silent, curious, alert. As they walk across neighborhood lawns, snow crunches under their boot heels and Liam thinks about the grass beneath it, wondering if, somewhere in its memory, a remnant of last spring remains. Banshee's labored breathing and the resigned calls of a passing flock of geese are the only sounds they hear. Beneath the horizon, the sun climbs from the night slowly, secretly, but it has not yet come.

The lake at the center of the park is iced over along the shore, gray-white, littered with the fallen branches of the aspens and oak and fir trees encircling it. In the middle of the lake, the ice grows opaque then clear, finally yielding to the frigid green water that refuses to freeze until next month. Liam studies the ice and the branches and the water and thinks about that same lake in summer. What a difference a few months can make. In summer, children sail toy boats, mothers push babies in strollers, teenagers bike and skateboard with headphones on their ears, and some old men fish along the banks while listening to the Rockies on the radio, never actually expecting a fish to hit on their lines. Then he thinks of the summer swans; the ones that so gracefully swim and duck their heads and nestle their beaks under their angelic, almost gossamer wings. Last summer, Liam watched them for hours on end, thinking about me, Plato, and seraphim in white.

"Do you know what Plato used to say about the swans, Rebecca?" he asks, sniffling with the cold.

She continues to walk, studying the leafless branch of an aspen a few feet in front of them. "No," she says. "I was never much of a philosophy gal." She pulls a branch from the aspen and breaks it open to smell inside.

"Well," Liam says. "You know how swans sing before they die? Like they know what's coming?"

She nods.

"I guess some people think they sing because they're in distress, upset that their lives are going to end. Not Plato. He said that swans never sing when they're upset. They don't sing when they're hungry, in danger, or injured, so why the hell would they start singing out of some kind of distress the last day of their lives? No, Plato said that was just people thinking that swans are like us, that they fear death like we do, and sing because they don't want to go. Plato said that's a bunch of bullshit. He thought the swans sing the day they die because they're filled with more joy that day than any other. They sing because they're expectant and ecstatic, because they know that something beautiful awaits them after they leave. That's why they sing loudest, most colorfully right before the end: they just can't wait. Plato thought the swan's final song was just their way of saying, 'C'mon'."

"Do you think he's right, Liam? That we should be anxious to go?" Rebecca asks, tossing the broken aspen branch on to the icy lake.

"I really don't know. I just hope when the time comes I'm not afraid, that I'm like the swans, like my brother, convinced there's something beautiful waiting for me on the other side. Someone—maybe Sean or Walt–keeps whispering to me that there *is* something beautiful waiting, but I don't know, I guess I'll just have to wait and see. I won't know until I get there. That used to piss me off quite a bit…the not knowing part…but at least I've got some people on the other side to help me, a little scouting party to show me the way. Regardless, I'm not ready for my swan song just yet. I got some living to do first."

They stop along the lake's edge and watch the sky. The sun is beginning to rise. A thin layer of gray clouds hugs the horizon, then begins to lift, like the sun beneath it is pushing it skyward. The light from the sun is visible before the sun itself. The underbelly of the clouds glows pink and purple and orange. Wine-colored canyons form and disappear as the gray-blue clouds roil across the horizon. Liam studies the point in the sky where the sun will rise and thinks of roses and dying embers, then a peach tree that used to grow in our Singer Street yard. Yes, the sky is the color of peaches and roses, wine and cotton candy. And Liam can't believe he hasn't seen this before, hasn't understood the sun as he does at this very moment. Incredulous, he giggles, because he realizes now that the sun isn't vindictive, malicious, or something to be feared, like he imagined in all of his stories, like Little Napoleon wanted him to believe. It doesn't have anything personally against him and it can't be defeated in a fight.

No, like Death, the sun includes everything indiscriminately, without favorites or malice. Stoic but bleeding, cold in its distance but afire in its heart, indifferent toward its supplicants but bursting to enliven them–the sun rises.

Banshee sees a squirrel race across the snow to a large pine and she bolts after it. Liam and Rebecca are pulled along behind her, working directly toward the sun, welcoming its warmth. As they jog after the dog, they see that the sun is now like an orange heart in the cerulean in which it floats, its burning edges bleeding into the gray-blue sky around it, sensually giving life to itself and a midwife to so many lives under it. Then the orange burns into a golden white and the sun inexorably climbs. And Liam's reminded that the sun is indifferent some times, begrudging at others. One minute it's hidden beneath a Southern California marine layer, the next burning your arm and the face of your brother as he lies dying in the high-desert dirt outside Temecula. But no matter its attitude or posture, its color or demeanor, the one thing that is constant is that each of us need it desperately, and if we're going to have any chance at living we've got to throw ourselves at its mercy.

Liam blinks then opens his eyes and looks directly into the heart of the sun. Its white rays drop languidly from it like flaming petals and Liam knows that the sun flowers all the time, you've just got to look at it, be awake and outside to see. The rays hurt his eyes and he feels the veins behind them pound, but he cannot look away, he's lost in it. Sunspots dance in his eyes and he's a little dizzy with the strength of the world around him. He blinks in a gesture of compliance to the sun and the sky, even though he cannot imagine all the things either of them contain, cannot understand all the things they know. And the fact that he can't control anything that matters doesn't bother him in the least.

He turns to Rebecca, "Do you see that? Look at the sun. It's like it's dropping things from the sky, like it's *flowering* somehow."

She looks at him and nods as if she sees it too and they begin to run toward it with their fingers entwined. Banshee picks up her pace, looks over her shoulder at them, and strides still faster. Liam feels lighter than he's felt in his whole life and knows that the burning of the stories has released him, has not only liberated him from a paper prison, but has destroyed the invisible, leaden chains he had no idea were locked around his legs. Little Napoleon is dead again and Liam feels weightless.

Still Rebecca and he run and grow lighter; the past disappearing, forgotten and left behind. Looking upward from the horizon, the color of the sky melts from lavender to pink to powder blue as the sun ascends. The sun rips completely free from the horizon, rising higher still. The contrast between this burning orb of life and the void of death grows more distinct as the morning progresses, but the sun is winning, and Liam, Rebecca, and Banshee are pulled toward it. They draw nearer and fear is a concept Liam can no longer fathom, control is something he willingly cedes.

The three of them run toward the terrifyingly beautiful mystery in the sky, and Liam screams, "C'MON."

And they begin to sprint.

Liam and Rebecca look at each other with eyes wide open and feel the pull of the beyond in their chests like a heavy palpitating flower. The sun seems to reach for them, its warm comforting fingers illumining their faces. The faster they run, the less their feet touch the ground. Then, incredibly, they sense the air expanding beneath their feet and the distance between their bodies and the ground growing. And because no uncompleted sorrow, no petty-ass dictators hold them back, because they're not afraid of falling– they fly into the sun. It asks no questions and wants nothing from them. It accepts them unblinkingly, like a brother.

So with the gum washed from his eyes, Liam accustoms himself to the dazzle of the light. And for the first time in a long time, he is alive again.

The End

About the Author

Patrick Hegarty is a writer living in California. The Dazzle of the Light is his first novel.

Lightning Source UK Ltd.
Milton Keynes UK
UKHW041838301022
411365UK00006B/18/J